COMMUNITY KILLING

A DI Huws Crime Thriller Book 1 of 3

ANNE ROBERTS

I dedicate this book to the memory of my late husband Mike Roberts. Writing and all things connected was his thing.

Chapter One

'OH GOD,' mumbled Dyfed as he rolled over and grabbed for his pager, flashing on the bedside cabinet, 'shit,' he thought as he knocked his mobile phone onto the floor and under the bed. He stumbled out of the bedroom trying not to disturb Elin and went into the bathroom to pull on his T shirt, and socks, grabbing a pair of trousers out of the laundry basket as he speed dialled the Ops room and made his way down stairs. His mouth felt like the bottom of a budgies cage as he asked what and where the job was.

This wasn't the first time he'd asked himself over the last few months if he was getting too old for this malarkey. The daytime call-outs were ok, being self-employed, he could always drop tools and go, but it seemed harder and harder with the night time jobs, his pager frequently waking him from a deep often troubled sleep, making his heart hammer in his chest and knocking him off kilter for a few minutes.

Hoover the Labrador wagged his tail against the kitchen cupboard from his basket in the corner, pleased to see him but too lazy to get up in the dead of night, knowing by now he wouldn't get much of a fuss. Grabbing his car keys, he closed the kitchen door behind him. He collected his overalls from the peg in the utility room, where he always kept them, easier to put on before his work boots. The rest of his gear lived in the back of his car, ready wherever he happened to be during the day should his pager sound.

It had been a busy season so far; the end of July and the beginning of August always were on his patch. He had a good team under him, so could always rely on a reasonable turnout of volunteer's day or night. Ten of them altogether, three old stagers, with a fair few years of service and used to all sorts, the others younger, twenties and thirties and not yet wise to the ways of the world. A couple of them not yet used to the slightly sick sense of humour that emanated out of the older team members. They would learn as time went on that it was purely a self-preserving mechanism employed by many like himself all over the UK.

Over the years on various training courses he had met a few older than himself who were exactly the same. Some had become quite cynical as the years went by, and Dyfed suspected it would be the case with the younger ones over time.

He was a good driver, not that he was legally allowed to break any speed limits in his own car, but regardless he usually did, particularly at night when the glare of oncoming traffic would alert him, however he needed to keep an eye out for the more nocturnal creatures. He'd really messed his van up one night when he hit a dog fox, he still felt guilty at not stopping to check it over, assuming the impact had killed it outright, but on driving back home later there was no sign of it. Either it had crawled, injured, to die somewhere, or somehow it had survived. Mind you, he thought, these modern car bumpers were such cheap, weak plastic that they withstood no bumping at all.

It was a beautiful moonlit night, that was one consolation, at least it was not raining , and being the end of August it was still warm, he looked at the outside temperature gauge, eighteen degrees, not bad, almost too warm for his fluorescents but he also knew that a long search could also coincide with a change in the weather, and the dawn could often bring a breeze, which combined with tiredness soon put a chill on you. He had been told by the Ops room to meet with police officers just to the south of the village of

Allt Goch, an area of shore popular at this time of year with visitors, where a long stretch of open bay ran around four miles long from end to end.

The terrain varied. Low cliffs and boulders on the east side, a large expanse of sandy beach for around a third of its length, where the visitor population tended to stay, a café and toilets for their convenience, and the odd camper van that stayed overnight on the grassy areas nearer the single-track road. Dyfed knew however that this was becoming a bit of an issue locally, the numbers, the litter, the countless motorhomes getting stuck on the steep hairpin bends causing friction.

From there, the beach became wider from the high tide mark to the sea, half of the distance made up of saltings and hundreds of sandy holes, mostly empty at this time of year, but often filled with water after the winter storms, where an onshore wind would push the high tide up towards the low-lying fields close to the shore. The water tended to stay in them once filled, debris pooled within and by the spring they tended to smell a bit rank. He had more than once in the dark heard his team mates fall into them, especially the ones where the marram grass had grown tall around them and hidden them during the day let alone at night. He had done it himself often enough as a youngster but knew by now that it was often a case of less speed more progress, or whatever the saying was.

The far end of the beach was technically the estuary mouth where the very silted up river emptied itself onto the vast wide expanse of beach, running out of steam as opposed to becoming any more powerful. The only time the river filled significantly was when the spring tides had the north easterlies behind them and pushed the river back from whence it came.

This area was treacherous as the tide came in, the beach was flat and wide, almost a mile and a half from the high, to low tide marks, causing the tide to move in at an alarming pace. He supposed it was a bit like the Morecambe sands, where all the poor cocklers got cut off and drowned. He had never been there himself but had heard stories from team members in that area that he'd met at the training school. Terrible it was by all accounts, the sounds of terror and lost hope without being able to get to them quickly enough.

He was the second of his team to arrive, Aled lived closer than he did, in fact probably no further than half a mile from where he farmed his smallholding. Despite his 'proper' job, as Aled called, being a self-employed accountant, Dyfed knew that Aled preferred his farming role. He was a dependable sort, good at dealing with the occasional slightly obnoxious person they came across. He had long ago accepted that not everyone was relieved at having been rescued, it depended entirely on how they had got themselves into the particular situation.

The police were there when he arrived, but only two of them in a panda car. 'Couldn't be anything big kicking off,' he thought to himself, then he saw the headlights of a couple more cars coming down the hill towards the beach, one would be the truck with all the search gear in and one of the other lads or indeed lass would be following on in their own car.

He'd been a coastguard for 22 years now so felt he had come across most things, but Aled who was already at the beach, had three years on him, and was the Station Officer, the head honcho in other words. Dyfed as deputy with no aspirations whatsoever to become the Station Officer himself, too much care and maintenance needed and mountains of paperwork which was never top of his agenda, although he was willing to help with anything that needed attention.

As a mechanic, Elin did all his book keeping and accounts and he just made sure he kept all the invoices and receipts in a box which she took away whenever she popped into the garage. Being a Maths teacher in the local secondary school had its uses but woe betide him if he didn't keep his receipts, or worse, if he allowed one to sit in the footwell of his car to disintegrate.

There were seven of them now at least. If the search area was this beach as he had been told, Aled may well need to ask the Ops room to mobilise a flank team – the next team along the coast, maybe the team each side would be needed if the situation warranted it. They all knew their adjacent patches reasonably well, particularly in the daytime, but night was a different story altogether.

Most of the team were kitted out now, yellows, helmets, life-jackets over their coats as per rules and a few of them with a small first aid kit slung over their shoulders. Torches in hand fully charged. No doubt a couple would have some Mars bars in their pockets – just in case it was a long job. The uniform was not the most comfortable to wear, sweat inducing at the best of times, and tonight would be no different.

Aled was talking to the Police, he stepped across to make sure they were all singing from the same hymn sheet with the right information.

Sometimes the police were a little sparse with the information they gave out, imparting as little as possible to get the job done, for instance – missing male, last seen at so and so and seen walking towards so and so, however tonight was not the same.

Sarah Jones, last seen at 4 p.m. having walked out of her home after a row with her parents, regarding her relationship with a lad they believed was very much beneath her social status. She was only fifteen and recently the sparks had been flying at home, more so since the school had told them at the end of the summer term that she had been absent frequently. The relationship had come to light and rows had started, particularly between the girl and her father.

The parents had issued the police with a good description, and unusually, a recent photo which was shared around for the team to see. They rarely got to see a picture of the missing person.

In most cases where young persons were reported missing, the parents would have covered all bases themselves before reporting their child missing. Often the Coastguard teams were not alerted until the said child had been missing for twenty-four hours or more. By the time all family members and friends had been exhausted and the police were alerted, there was time for them to be well away.

The parents didn't have a phone number for the boyfriend, but on naming him, he was known to the police, petty burglaries mainly, but also known to dabble in the fringes of the world of hard drugs. Not a major player or supplier, but a wanabee. He had been turfed out of his bed 2 a.m. but disappointingly there was no evidence of Sarah having spent the evening with him. Also being twenty-seven, he denied any liaison with Sarah beyond hanging out with her and her mates a few times.

More information was then dished out, the clothes she was last seen in, and the style she had her hair in when she stormed out, a pony tail tied low down at the nape of her neck, a pair of silver loop earrings in her ears, and much to her parent's dislike, a nose stud. However, the most important part of the information came at the end, that Sarah was diabetic and as she had grown up into her teenage years had become disdainful and neglectful of her condition and tried her best to ignore it.

As far as her parents were concerned, she had left the house with no money and no snacks, so by now her blood sugar could be critically low and in danger of causing a hypoglycaemic episode, this was the main reason the police had responded so quickly as opposed to their occasional, 'Let's give them twenty-four hours.'

Chapter Two

'CAN YOU GATHER AROUND FOR A MINUTE?' said Aled. By now he had asked the ops room for more information with regards to tide times and had been told that high tide was at 6:30 a. m. It was currently 3:45 a.m. so they had a bit of time to make sure they swept the main beach area before the tide covered it. Day break would be roughly 5:30 a.m. but the fact that the expanse of beach covered ten square miles made Aled ask the Ops room to page the flank teams so that they could conduct at least a hasty search of the area before high tide, then a more concentrated grid search could be carried out later on. It would take a while for the teams to get there, so Aled needed to organise the team he had and get them started.

'Ok, let's get you splitting into three teams for now. John stay with the truck and maintain comms, don't overdo the radio stuff, and clog the channel as there'll soon be a fair few of us out here. Her mobile has been pinged to this area but now the tracing has been lost so she has either taken the sim out or God forbid, something has happened to her and her phone. Please report Obs Normal as a welfare check every twenty minutes. Her mates have somehow got wind that she was over this way, so keep an eye out. If any of them are doing their own thing they need to be aware of the tide and any soft sand areas, we don't want it becoming a mud rescue job as well. Has anyone bought any chocolate with them?'

'I have' said Ceri, 'You know me boss, always prepared for a long job and thinking of my belly.'

'Ok,' said Aled, 'If we find her pretty soon, we can get something sweet down her as long as she is conscious, so just remember your first aid protocols, recovery position, warmth and all that, so don't eat the chocolate Ceri.'

'Yup ok,' yawned Ceri, still half asleep, probably had a late night, as the youth of today seemed to do.

Dyfed was paired with David. David was the only English member of the team, being a very Welsh rural area, most of the locals were first language Welsh, they always spoke Welsh to each other, but when David was present, English was spoken out of good manners. David was a secondary school teacher in the local comprehensive school five miles outside the village of Allt Goch. Most of the local children were bussed there and back daily. David was easy to chat to and Dyfed always enjoyed their conversations. It was good to have an intelligent conversation beyond football and rugby, which apart from women, was the daily topic of conversation between the two lads he employed at the workshop.

By now there was a slight hint of light to the east, but not enough to see clearly without their torches. The three teams were spaced at intervals across the width of the bay and he could see the torch lights of his colleagues making regular sweeps around themselves.

Aled and Michael had ended up nearest the sea, conscious all the time of the incoming tide and also aware of all the little gulley's and dips, in what looked like a flat expanse of beach. It was easy to get cut off as the rising tide sneaked in behind you, but they knew the beach well. Michael was the pub landlord and for his sins was also a local councillor, he knew virtually everyone in the village as his little pub was a bit of a central hub. Many local clubs met at the village, the chess club, creative writing gathering, after choir eating place, and even more recently a knitting club. It enabled him to keep his ear to the ground and know what was going on, good and sometimes bad, in the locality.

Dyfed and David had the central position searching the land-ward edge of the sand and the edge of the saltings. A fairly easy walk crossing the narrow mouths of many a small hillside stream emptying pathetically onto the sand. In winter these could be raging torrents, gouging great channels in the sand and making their way directly into the sea. The beach landscape was ever changing with growing and receding saltings dependent on the winter weather.

Ceri and Tomos had drawn the short straw tonight, being the youngest they had been allocated the trickiest territory, right across the saltings up to the sea wall. No doubt there would be wet feet before morning. They would have a hard time, no chance for banter. Dry ankle twisting ditches hid at every step, and some streams which had cut deep chasms which needed jumping with accuracy and agility, not easy in your yellows and steel toe capped boots.

Dyfed's radio crackled, the comms were not particularly good in the bay with both area masts well out of direct line, so all local communication needed to be through the Coastguard vehicles radio system which would relay messages, from the teams on the ground to the Ops room. The radio was responding to one of the flank team members notifying of their arrival at the west end of the beach, with five on board, so again two teams of two, and one to stay with their truck to relay positions and progress to all concerned.

The police were not in contact other than by land line from their headquarters with the Coastguard Ops room in nearby Holy-head, so there was often a bit of delay in communications, but this was nothing unusual.

Dyfed heard a familiar sound approaching from the south, a view obscured as yet by the hill rising behind the beach, but he recognised it as the local Search and rescue helicopter which had been requested to assist. They had heat seeking equipment on board but were still going to have a tough job covering such a huge area. Normally they worked it in grid squares as they did when searching over the sea. Progress along the sand was fairly hasty, but he was aware of the torch lights to his left trailing behind, just because the terrain prevented his team mates from making quick progress.

The order had been to make a hasty search initially, and then when the whole beach had been covered, to retrace their steps, but in what was termed a Grid search formation, a little like what you would see police search teams doing following something like a murder, maybe not quite a fingertip search but close enough. By the time they were ready to start that, the second flank team would no doubt have arrived and be organised to join them, and hopefully be a little fresher. There may even be a couple more of his own team turning up, Gareth for instance worked nights until 6 a.m. but had been known to turn up at a search for a couple of hours before collapsing into bed at lunchtime for a few hours kip before his night shift started again at 6 p.m.

Dyfed loved the dawn, everything starting to wake up, bright rays of light starting to appear through the forest on the hillside which gradually crept further and further across the beach, like arrows of light spearing towards the sand. He always thought on days like this, that he really ought to make the effort to get up this early every summers day, but somehow, it never seemed to happen, and seven o'clock always seemed early enough, especially if he had not had a decent night's sleep, which was quite often the case these days.

6 a.m. and his team mates were making good progress, the teams nearest the sea's edge were rapidly reaching each other, being a fairly easy walk, keeping their eyes on the rapidly incoming tide, they were mainly walking on an angle towards the shore. Soon the beach would be covered, and no doubt the nearby inshore lifeboat would be called upon to search. Later after the tide had gone out, a second search by the coastguard to cover the sand newly exposed, just in case of anything washed ashore, which had been in the sea. The coastguard helicopter had by now been and gone with nothing found.

Life was returning to the beach with the dawn light, the cackle of gulls overhead, keeping a beady eye on the sea for mackerel and whitebait which was plentiful at this time of year, though in his opinion, gulls were now lazy bastards who preferred to hang around town and snatch sandwiches and ice creams out of the clutches of the unsuspecting visitors. Some days it was like an episode of Hitchcock's 'The Birds'. It was people's own fault largely, they were too lazy often to walk to a bin, so threw the fish and chip cartons on the floor, seaside towns and villages had become easy pickings for gulls. They could be quite vicious too, particularly when the young hatched in the rooftop nests, and they started early flying lessons. They had been known to land on people's shoulders with a nasty peck.

The cattle in the fields adjoining the sea wall were lying down in a group chewing their cud, not perturbed in the least by the activity on the beach.

The coastal path actually went along the sea wall at this point, so they were used to seeing the odd locals and visitors walking along. On the seaward side the wall was almost ten-foot-high to its five foot on the landward side. A few years before, the local council had built a solid railed fence along the top of the wall to stop people falling off it. They still had the odd faller though, who had caught a foot in the fields wire fence which formed the inner edge, one person had gone head first into the field and broken their leg. Luckily nowadays most people carry a mobile phone. It hadn't been an easy job stretchering them to the road access, through the deep tractor ruts and cow muck that had built up over the winter.

Ceri and Tomos were now three quarters of the way along the beach, having got to slightly easier terrain, the flank team members had also covered the other end and were probably within three hundred metres of Ceri and Tomos now. Once the teams met and were sure they had done a decent job, they'd normally have a short break for refreshment, or a cigarette, which was the case with a couple of the team members, and then restart the search from one end, but everyone arranged in a line closer together to start the grid search. This would cover the ground in far more detail and leave no stone unturned.

All the team members came together at 6:30 a.m. at the original rendezvous point, some decidedly wet and dirty by now, after the odd trip and fall into the many holes in the saltings. Ceri was wet from the waist down and didn't mind everyone hearing her complain loudly about it, though Aled preferred if she didn't swear quite so much. Another local team had now joined, so at least they had a few fresh people to give them a hand. Aled sent Ceri and Tomos home, secretly glad that Tomos had come in his own car and could give Ceri a lift home to save soaking the seats in the coast-guard truck. They may both be needed again later if the police decided to keep them searching the area.

Chapter Three

'COME HERE YOU LITTLE BUGGER,' shouted Richard, as he strode along the woodland path, well-trodden now compared to years gone by, because the local council had decided to assign it a footpath. It never used to be, in his youth, in fact, it had simply been a route that locals would have walked to move between smallholdings in the area. He remembered as a boy how he had once walked behind his parents following a coffin, held high on the shoulders of a group of neighbours, bringing the body of someone's dearly departed from their home to the local church higher up the hill. It was the way things were done then.

He whistled again to no avail, what the hell had made him choose a Jack Russell terrier after his last faithful lab had died of old age, he didn't know, however he was in the main a good dog, if a bit wilful. It was easy to lose him in these woods, but he would always appear from somewhere with a muddied snout, no doubt having been poking around in some sort of hole in the ground. Today he was slower in coming back, but he always did, so Richard walked on ahead.

His attention had been drawn this early morning to the activity going on down at the beach as the sun was rising, the sound of a helicopter hovering nearby during the night suggesting something was amiss. Some poor sod in trouble out at sea no doubt, he thought, when he had recognised the people as the local coastguard team members.

He knew some of the crew, Dyfed who attended to his old car and somehow kept it mechanically sound, and David who taught at his grandsons' school and of course Aled who lived just at the other end of the woodland. They did a good job, called out all hour's day or night.

He whistled again as he started to make his way slightly down-hill, aware all the time of the protruding tree roots that could easily trip him up. Margaret his wife always checked he had his mobile phone with him before he left the house, after an incident the summer before last, when he had fallen and badly twisted his ankle. No one found him for ages as he had not taken his phone or told anyone which one of the hundreds of local forestry and woodland tracks he was walking. In fact, that time it was the dog arriving home before him that alerted Margaret to anything being wrong, and she eventually organised a search party from amongst the neighbours. It had taken him up to last spring to really get over the ligament damage and be able to enjoy his long walks again.

He could hear Scot yapping now and snarling. He must have come across something that didn't seem to please him very much, a fox maybe, it wasn't beyond him to get caught up in a fight with a fox or the odd dog. That was the problem with these terriers, they thought they were bigger than any other dog.

Scot came into view; he was certainly having a good bark at something, and in turn going forwards into the undergrowth then reversing in haste. 'It will just be a hedgehog' he thought to himself, as he recalled seeing him do that one evening in the garden when he has let him out for a last pee and a sniff around. 'Come away you daft thing,' he called to no avail, not even a glance in his direction. He realised in a few metres that Scot was just above the entrance of one of the two caves that were on the hillside. He had no real idea what their origins were, some said they were natural structures, others that they were part of a network of old mine workings from some ancient age or another, history had never been his strong point, he was more a science scholar.

He did use to play in them as a child though, if he was out with his mates on a rainy day. The one that Scot stood by now was the best cave, quite a drop down into the entrance hole, which was a bit of a squeeze for an adult but easy for a smaller child, and once in, it opened up so they could comfortably stand up. It had been a great adventure to come in here with some borrowed candles and a couple of comics. They had even got a couple of old blankets to sit on. He smiled to himself as he reminisced.

He soon had the smile wiped off his face. Scot stepped back when Richard got to him, as if he had done his job, pointing out his find, Richard almost stumbled over in shock as he looked at his dog's discovery, immediately turning away and vomiting into the undergrowth. He never did have a strong stomach, and what he saw now shocked him to the core.

He stumbled back, grasping at the sapling next to him, which bent under his weight as he fell sideways and slithered a couple of feet down the slope, Scot was going berserk now in his excitement, more to do with Richard's behaviour than what he had found, he danced around Richard yapping and wagging his tail at this new game, with no inclination whatsoever of the enormity of what was going on. Richard recovered his feet, but half fell, half staggered a few feet away from the cave entrance. Grabbing at his jacket pocket, feeling for the weight of his mobile phone, he fumbled and got it out, punching the emergency number into it, he could barely breathe. \

'What service do you require?' asked the voice.

'I don't know,' rasped Richard, 'Umm Police, maybe ambulance?'

'Ok Sir,' said the voice as they proceeded to ask him to calm down, while he put him through to the local police call centre who asked him where he was.

'Bloody hell, I don't know how to explain,' he told them, 'I'm in the woods, above the bay, I haven't got a grid reference, I don't need one, I know my way around.' He explained as best he could, and suggested the best access point for them, by coming down the Wern road and taking a right towards the farm, going off then along the footpath on the right, half way down.

He put the phone down and tried to gather his wits about him. As he clipped Scot onto his lead, the dog quite subdued by now, Richard didn't quite know how he felt. The initial rush of adrenaline had died down, allowing him to think a little more logically, however there was no way on earth he was going to be able to look in the cave entrance again. He had seen enough the first time. He could feel his heart hammering in his chest as he walked towards a moss-covered boulder and sat himself down.

They had told him to stay where he was, and they would call as they got to the woodland entrance, and that he should call back so they could find him. They shouldn't take long. He was shaking, and still felt waves of nausea washing over him. He looked down through the trees and through a gap saw that the coastguard teams on the beach were being picked up by their vehicles and making off towards the eastern end of the beach, no doubt in order to return to the road and go up the hill back towards Allt Goch. Must have been a training exercise, bit early though he thought, not for a minute connecting what he had just found with their presence.

The sun was out now, the sky blue, but he was chilled through to the bone. Scot whined; no doubt bored now of being made to sit still. Richard thought he would start making his way back the way he came, at least to the little bridge over the stream. There was a bungalow there, he knew the couple who lived there by sight, nice couple, they might spare him a tot of brandy, he could certainly do with it to calm his nerves and maybe warm him up inside. He had been told by a relative once that alcohol didn't really warm you up, that was a false feeling, but at this very moment in time he honestly didn't care.

He pulled at Scot's lead, and went to turn away, just as a big crow flew down through the canopy and landed just by the cave entrance, a bloody hoody crow, that explained what he had seen earlier, damn them, carrion eating filth. He rushed forwards waving his arms, just enough to cause it to fly away, as he turned again, Scot was yapping, and wagging his tail excitedly, he could hear voices. Damn it he thought, he hadn't phoned Margaret, but no time for that now, the voices must be the police.

'Over here,' he shouted, surprising himself with the weakness and hoarseness of his voice. 'Keep coming, I 'm down this way.' He half walked, half ran towards the voices, thinking, the sooner he directed them the sooner he could go home.

Three officers came towards him, and another in a suit, he introduced himself. 'Detective Inspector Idris Huws,' he said, 'I'm assuming you are the first informant? Will you show me where she is please?'

'Over there,' said Richard, 'I'm not going anywhere near the place, I've seen enough to have nightmares for years to come, terrible, terrible, who could have done such a thing, and here? Nothing bad ever happens here.' He felt himself getting hysterical now, not really like him at all.

'Thank you, Sir, if you go with Sergeant Pritchard here, he will take you back to the road and drive you to the station.'

'The station? Why? Why do I need to go to the Police Station? I need to go home and tell Margaret what's happened, she'll be worried.'

The DI looked at him with a look on his face that Richard found difficult to read, but he wasn't sure he liked what he saw.

'One of my officers has already gone down to your home and is with your wife now, she knows you are not hurt, but we will need to ask you some questions.'

The third officer was now winding blue and white tape around the trees in the vicinity of the cave entrance.

'My God,' thought Richard, 'this only happens to people on television.' He was worried about Margaret; she wasn't long home from hospital after a mild stroke. He followed the young sergeant, Scot, pulling ahead at the excitement of all the new people.

'Hey what about my dog?' asked Richard.

'Oh, he will be fine with me, I love dogs,' said the sergeant who Richard reckoned was about fifteen. They got younger and younger it seemed.

'I'll run him back to your house when we have got you sorted at the station, don't worry it shouldn't take long, just a few questions, and fingerprints-'

'What did you say? Fingerprints? What on earth for? I haven't done anything, I just phoned to tell the police what I had found.'

'It's just procedure Sir, don't worry about it.'

Chapter Four

DYFED UNDID his laces and kicked off his boots, stepping into the kitchen. Hoover met him at the door with an old sock in his mouth, a present. Dyfed smiled and rubbed his head, 'Hi old boy, had your walk?'

'You talk to the dog before you talk to me,' said Elin with a smile on her face. 'If you had texted to say you were on your way, I could have had breakfast ready for you.'

'Sorry love, didn't think.'

'What was it, false alarm, a hoax?' she asked getting some bits and pieces out of the fridge.

'No, I don't think so, something genuine I reckon, missing girl. They must have found her though as we were called off. No word yet though but I reckon she was with a friend, trouble at home because of boys apparently.'

He sat down, glad to rest his feet for a minute, he would have a bite and then get off to work, his lads were used to him by now, they were a good pair and would get on with their work till he arrived.

Dyfed and the Coastguards in general were rarely told by the police what the result of these types of searches were, and in fact the first they would hear would often be in the Daily paper the next day. In cases like this 'mispers' as they were referred to – missing persons, it generally turned out to be a family feud of one sort or another and nothing more was heard. He said goodbye to Elin, gave her a peck on the cheek and closed the door behind him, and off he went to do his normal working day.

Aled sat at the big pine table, coffee cup in hand, Jo his wife clearing away the breakfast dishes. He had a lot planned for today, the first job would be late to start now but would get done. He had another cut to make in the top fields, it was only five acres but a good number of silage bales again to add to the completed stack for the winter. He had fertilised this year, something he hadn't bothered with the last few years – the cost of the stuff was going up year by year, but he had cottoned on to the fact that he had a ready market for surplus bales amongst some of the local horse owning community. There were loads of horses and ponies around these parts, he supposed having beach, forestry and miles of country lanes made riding an attractive hobby.

He would get going with that in a minute, after he had checked his post and e-mails, after all it was his accountancy work that helped him pay for the pleasure of living where, and how they did. It worked well, their lives had changed so much since moving full time to this glorious area of North Wales.

He had spent most of his adult life to date, working for a large accountancy company on the edge of Manchester, and Jo had been a primary school teacher. They fell in love with the area on one of their many short breaks in the locality, and when they found Bryn Gwyn Bach advertised it was love at first sight, plus the price had been very un-refusable. It had needed a lot of work and it was registered by a Welsh Preservation Society so they were limited to what they could do outside, but the inside was now beautifully renovated, and for a very old property, it was actually quite contemporary, and shocked many first-time visitors by its lightness and spaciousness compared to the image expected from the outside.

They had sold their Manchester suburbs house, where he had to admit he knew no one, not even his next- door neighbour. It had allowed them to buy Bryn Gwyn Bach, mortgage free and also have money left over to do it up. They had managed to buy the cottage twenty- five years previously and had been in the lucky position to be able to continue to live, and earn in Manchester, and do up the cottage whilst renting a small flat. In fact, he had moved here permanently way before Jo could give up her teaching position.

Jo did not miss her teaching job, having been unable to get a position in such a strong Welsh language stronghold, she'd instead put all her efforts into helping Aled with the project of renovating the house and outbuildings, and helped him when needed with paperwork. She had however, been invited with open arms into the community, and always had something on the go at the village hall.

They had a small flock of pedigree Dartmoor sheep, tough little buggers who coped easily with the relatively mild Anglesey winters. They were lucky that the land was sheltered, dry in comparison with the general area, and they wintered out with very little supplementary feed. It was mainly a breeding herd, the lambs generally sold off to other smallholder hobby breeders. Jo never liked the idea of eating them, her own fault for giving the ewes names.

Today, he also had the first couple of clients bringing their accounts for the once over, before their end of October deadline for self- assessment tax returns. It was very different here from Manchester's organised paperwork. Many of his clients simply bought him carrier bags full of receipts and invoices, expecting him to do all the sorting and book keeping, and then working out their dues. It took hours, and they still whinged at the bill at the end of the day.

Jo had been and fed their small flock of hens and returned in with a bowl full of eggs, brown white and blue from some fancy breed she had insisted on buying at the Royal Welsh winter fair last year. She used most of the eggs herself, baking and cooking but loved to be able to hand out half a dozen when friends visited.

'What's going on in the woods today?' she asked, 'seems to be loads of voices coming from there'.

'Haven't a clue,' Aled barely turned his head from the computer screen in front of him.

'I think I will take a stroll and have a look' said Jo.

'Ok, I'll just see what's on here then I'm going to get the mower out and get cutting, I should be finished for a late lunch, if I get on with it now.'

After a quick check through e mails, and deciding there was nothing urgent, Aled closed down the computer and changed into his work boots, stuck his favourite check shirt over his T shirt and walked over to the shed where the tractor was kept. The new shed was really the only addition to the place since they had moved in. A modern agricultural building housing the tractor and the few implements he had gathered together, the mower, topper, harrows, roller and fertilizer spinner, all bought second hand at local farm auctions. He had a few pens in here too, for the ewes when they lambed. They didn't ever plan the lambing until March, unlike the Christmas lambs he often saw hereabouts. He loathed to see two and three-day old lambs huddling and shivering, in the awful weather that December to February could throw at them.

He had built the shed close to the house, for night time check convenience, having learnt their lesson the second year they were there when they lost more than their fair share to a local fox population from lambing the flock outdoors.

He had been lucky to source his tractor, a not too huge Massey Ferguson, four-wheel drive model, as rare as hens' teeth apparently, front loader and everything for handling the bales through the winter. He delivered the odd bale locally, as most of the local horse owners had no means of transporting or moving them into place, and only wanted one at a time.

He filled the tractor with diesel and hopped into the cab. He even had a radio to listen to, mind you he would do better to concentrate on what he was doing.

Jo walked to the end of their drive, more a track really. She loved it, still grass growing in the middle along its length, mind you some of their more townie visitors didn't appreciate it with their low-slung cars, some even parked them at the entrance and walked to the farm, easily a half mile walk. They weren't always best pleased, dependent on their choice of shoes, but they had been warned and most forgot about their discomfort when they entered what they saw as a slightly ruinous old cottage, to see the beautifully designed Scandi style interior. Spacious and light, the huge inglenook filling one end with a full height ceiling.

The track ended at a kissing gate on their boundary and continued as a pathway through unkempt old woodland. In fact, the fields next door were involved in some family dispute or another over ownership and access and had not been grazed as far as she knew, for over twenty years and were now liberally dotted with over ten-year-old self- sown saplings.

At this time of year, the path was barely used, being so over-grown, only the dedicated local walkers pushing their way through the long grass bracken and nettles. Once through the overgrown field which extended to her right, over the shoulder of the hill, you entered a slightly denser area of woodland, which had a clear path through to the little hamlet beyond. Her favourite time of year was the spring, which gave the woods their local name of Bluebell woods. There was a huge acreage of wild unclaimed land in the immediate area, probably two to three hundred acres of wilderness to a certain degree in all. None of it currently farmed, though some effort was being made at the top of the hill to reclaim an old farm-stead, where the long-time residents had died, and the property had been left to someone outside the area. Good luck to them, thought Jo, it would take a pretty penny to get it workable and productive again.

She could hear voices again now, but not well enough to make out what was going on, but as she was about to drop down a little slope to cross a small stream, she was stopped in her tracks. Blue and white coloured tape hung across the path and then she spotted the back of a police officer.

'What's going on?' she asked. The young policeman had obviously had his mind elsewhere and not heard her approach, as he tried to disguise his surprise and blocked her path.

'I'm sorry madam, I can't allow you to continue along this path today, we have some work going on here and the footpath is blocked until further notice.'

'Oh, I live just across the field in the farm at the end of the track, I was alerted by voices and wondered if maybe someone was lost, what's happened?'

'I'm sorry I'm not at liberty to say, and in fact will have to ask you to return the way you came and leave the area.'

'But-'

'I'm sorry Madam, I don't make the rules,' he was polite, but it was pretty obvious from his manner he meant what he said, there was no going for a nosey for her. Just as she was about to turn away, she caught a glimpse of another person about a hundred metres ahead, in a white coverall head to toe.

Obviously, something not so nice had happened. She turned back and retraced her steps to the farm. It was pointless either ringing or texting Aled, he wouldn't hear above the sound of the machinery, she would have to walk to the top field to tell him. She noticed as she emerged in a clearing that there was a helicopter approaching from the south easterly direction, over the crest of the hill at the other end of the beach, making its way in her direction. She recognised it as a police helicopter from the local force as opposed to the search and rescue helicopter that had been about in the early hours. Aled saw the helicopter too but paid it no heed as he set off on the next row of sward to be cut.

Chapter Five

RICHARD DRANK the last dregs of the coffee he had been given by the young officer. His hands having only just stopped shaking from the shock of the find this morning. He knew Margaret had arrived at the station, as he had heard her voice, but as yet he had not been allowed to see her. He had only been allowed to have a pee, after explaining that his old bladder wasn't as reliable as it had been, before the joys of the old water tablets that were prescribed to him, they were a total pain, and dictated totally his movements for a few hours through the morning, until their effect had worn off, but they were doing their job, he supposed alongside the rest of the concoction that he took for his dodgy ticker.

The door opened, and the same young officer walked in. 'You are free to leave Sir, but we may well need to talk to you again at some point in our enquiries.'

'But you haven't asked me anything?' exclaimed Richard.

'No, it's ok Sir, we have verified your whereabouts this morning through a couple of witnesses, so you are free to go.'

'Thank God for that, I could do with a sit down in my own chair, with a tot of whisky in my hand.'

'I'm sure Sir, thank you for your time this morning, but you have to understand we have to dot the I's and all that.'

Margaret was by the front desk when he left the room, she stepped forwards and squeezed his hand. 'Come on love, let's get you in the car and home, you have had a terrible time by the sound of it.'

He got in the passenger side of the car and belted. Margaret, did most of the driving these days, it had become the norm since he had badly injured his leg, though there had been a slight question about her still doing so, after the stroke. It was however deemed so mild; she was allowed to continue. Richard put his head in his hands and rubbed his eyes.

'I'm speechless,' he said. 'I have no words for what I have saw. I doubt I'll ever get the vision out of my minds-eye ever again. Makes me sick to the stomach to think about it, the poor love. Who the hell around here would do such a thing to another human being?'

'Forget it now for a bit Love, let's just get you in the house. Though whether we can get down our road I don't know, the place was crawling with police cars and vans, parked everywhere when I drove up the hill. They had to park on the road and walk down the track to get to the entrance of the woods, and the top of the track is all taped off with policemen standing guard. It must be those scenes of crime people like you see on TV because a few of them were in overalls with gloves and facemasks on.'

Richard sat in silence for the remainder of the short drive home, he felt that if he said or thought too much, he would burst into tears, like a child. Sure enough as they came to the junction at the top of their road in the village, there was a police car parked. They stopped, and after a brief chat, Margaret was allowed to drive on towards home.

'I had to get the postman to vouch for you being at home this morning, and Peter and Diane told them they had seen you pass their house and turn into the woods at whatever time they saw you, they must have been happy with that information.'

'Hmm,' answered Richard, 'Still managed to make me feel like a criminal when in fact I was a victim to have had to see what I did.'

He slammed the car door, going in through the back door where Scot met him happily wagging his tail. 'Hey old boy, come on let's go through and sit down. You've seen horrors today as well haven't you?' He slumped into his chair, and breathed a sigh of relief at being home, but he noticed his hands tremoring, as Margaret passed him a welcome glass of malt.

The phone rang in the kitchen, he heard Margaret answer it, then obviously close the door so as not to disturb him, or else prevent him from hearing the conversation. She needn't have worried, along with his other aches and pains, his hearing wasn't the best now either. Margaret entered the room.

'That was Jo, Aled's wife, she wanted to know what the police were doing in the woods and thought maybe we would have seen or heard something at this end. Aled was trying to finish the top fields and asked her to phone. I told her what you said you found; I hope I haven't done wrong. Horrified she was and a bit scared, she's gone back to tell Aled.'

'Ah well, no doubt everyone will know something soon anyway, once the newspaper reporters get hold of this sort of thing, they'll be here in their droves.' He stopped at this point as if this fact had only just entered his head. 'Oh, for God's sake if anyone comes snooping around here asking questions tell them I have nothing to say to them.' He finished off his glass of whisky and shouted, 'Another.' His head fell back, and he closed his eyes, trying hard, but failing to obliterate the terrible visions playing out inside his eyelids, like the worst horror film ever.

Aled could see Jo running up between the rows of cut grass. Something must be up, he thought, his Jo didn't usually run anywhere for anybody. Being slightly chubby as she liked to describe herself, she was no cross-country runner, as her bright red face proved when she reached him. He stopped the engine as she bent down hands on knees catching her breath.

'There's been a murder,' she blurted out. 'In our wood's, a young woman, according to Margaret.' Jo gasped to draw in her breath. 'Worst of all, it was Richard who found her, walking the dog early this morning, he's only just back from the police station in Bangor now.'

She gulped noisily again as Aled said, 'Do we know who she is?' A horrible thought had immediately put two and two together in his head. The young girl they had been searching for earlier, the search had been called off with no explanation from the police, much as happened normally. His team had all gone home and about their daily business, and the poor girl had been found by Richard no more than a field away from the farm.

'No, I don't think Margaret or Richard knew that.'

'That's terrible. Come on I'll come down to the house with you, could do with a cuppa, I will phone Richard myself and see what's going on, but murder? Here? that's too much to imagine. Who the hell would be capable of doing something like that? Nothing ever happens here apart from a petty burglary, a chainsaw or strimmer from an unlocked shed. Come on.'

His mobile rang, it was Michael from the pub in the village, one of his buddies from the Coastguard team. Like himself, Michael would have gone home from the search this morning straight back to whatever needed doing at the pub, or no doubt about it, he would be attending some meeting or another at the local council offices in the nearest town. He was tempted to ignore the call, in favour of looking after Jo who was clearly upset.

'Hi,' he said. 'Yes, I've just heard, who told you about it?' He listened nodding his head at whatever was being said. 'Right ok, will let you know if I hear any more, bye.'

'I can't believe this is happening so close to us here, we moved from Manchester, to get away from stuff like this,' said a tearful Jo.

Chapter Six

DYFED PICKED up his mobile phone from the work bench, he glanced at the screen, it was Aled.

'Hi, have you heard anything from this morning's job yet?' he asked before Aled could say anything.

'No mate, not as such, but a young girl's body has been found in the woods, not too far away from me here. Mutilated apparently, but I'm not wanting to make assumptions. It's likely it's the young girl we were looking for.'

'Oh shit,' said Dyfed, then turned to the entrance of the back office so the lads couldn't hear him. 'Do you mean she's been murdered? Here in Allt Goch?'

'I'm not saying that,' said Aled, 'I'm just telling you what I've heard, the police are there now, no doubt we will all hear something soon on the news, the area is all taped off. Jo went over there to see what all the voices were and got sent away with a flea in the ear. I'll let you know if I find anything more. Old Richard down the hill found her, or rather his dog did, dead upset he is too obviously, let me know if you hear anything.'

· · ·

Dyfed disconnected the call, then as quickly, dialled Elin's mobile number and repeated what he had been told. She was speechless and told Dyfed she would let him know if she heard something, but that would be unlikely. 'That's not why I'm telling you,' he said, 'if this is a murder then whoever has done it is still out there, come straight here from work and I will close up early and go home at the same time as you, I don't want you to be alone.'

Word soon got out amongst the local residents; the phone lines were hot with people trying to get any news. Jungle drums. It was a big story in the area, nothing like this ever happened in this small corner of Wales since a henpecked husband clobbered his wife with an iron, killed her and buried her in the sands of Red Wharf Bay. That was way back in 1945 though. A long time ago now. The conclusion had already been made that it was the young missing girl Sarah Jones.

Ceri Thomas picked up her mobile, it was John her Coastguard colleague.

'Fucking hell,' she said after a couple of seconds listening. 'Remind me never to get a bloody dog, it's always dog walkers that find this sort of thing, isn't it?' she said. 'Poor girl, is it definitely her?'

She stayed on the phone only another second and couldn't switch it off fast enough to phone Tomos, who had also been on the search job with her.

He responded with stunned silence.

'Where did John hear this?'

'Everyone seems to know,' she answered, 'The old boy that lives at the bottom of the hill the other end of the forest found the body this morning when he was out walking his dog,' she spoke as if it was the most exciting thing that had ever happened to her.

'Hmm, probably while we were still out on the beach looking. No wonder we were stood down with no real explanation.'

Chapter Seven

DI HUWS HAD ALWAYS, and would always, hate the building in the local hospital that housed the morgue and the autopsy room. His very first attendance at a P.M, had been as a young constable, and that was a local sudden death with what was thought then to be suspicious circumstances. He had worked very hard to fight back the nausea, and failed dismally, to his embarrassment. It was always the smell. A lingering, cloying, thick sort of smell that you couldn't get out of your nostrils for hours after it was all done and dusted.

A young colleague of his at the time, had told him he needed to plug his nostrils with Vicks inhaler, just before he went into the room, which he duly did. Oh yes, certainly it helped block out the smell, but by god, his eyes ran so much that he couldn't see what was going on, he spent the time with a hanky wiping his eyes and denying that he was weeping at the procedure in front of him. He hadn't done that again in a hurry. Nor had he been allowed to forget it either, his mates at the time nick naming him Vick, thankfully it didn't follow him to his next station. Now he tended to just be a little heavy handed with a spray bottle of aftershave, he kept in his car for these occasions. Over time he had hardened a little to the procedure.

The Pathologist, was just putting on his overalls and gloves, as he arrived much as a surgeon would do in a theatre with a live person to work on. The body was laid in front of a glass screened area still covered with a sheet. Thankfully, nowadays he was separated by the screen, in another room with full view, and a speaker to communicate, state of the art apparently, being the only large hospital facility for many miles, all autopsies in the area were done here.

Earlier that day he had escorted the young girls' distraught parents to view and identify the body, not an easy task considering the attack that had taken place on her body, her face was thankfully intact, but her neck had to be very carefully hidden from their view. She had been identified as 15-year-old Sarah Jones.

Now, the task of finding the cause of death, would start in detail. Very little helpful evidence having been found at the scene, although they were still working there, and that would continue for a while yet, it was hoped that more information would become apparent during the post mortem. Idris Huws certainly hoped so, they needed to get this particular perpetrator behind bars as soon as possible, considering how they had attacked this poor girl's body.

It had become clear from talking to the parents, that the row they had was a heated one, and Sarah had walked out. Her mother had wanted to go after her, but Steven Jones her father had insisted that she would not go far and would be back sulking soon enough. How wrong he had been. Mrs Jones was now totally distraught that the last communication she had with her daughter, had been bitter words between them, accusatory words, horrible words that she would have done anything to be able to take back.

In cases like this he found that often the tragedies broke up families, the grief, the pain, leading to accusations, and blame, and often ending with divorce courts. He was thankful he rarely had to deal with cases like this in his small, quiet patch of Wales.

Rowlands, the pathologist drew back the sheet, he had a tendency to drama, causing Huws to hold his breath, not really wanting to take in the scene in front of him. What he saw was a repeat of the nightmare scene that had faced him in the forest. The young victim was laid on her back, her hair tidily pulled back behind her, but streaked with mud. Her throat was a gaping open wound such as he had not seen before, this was no knife wound, her throat structures described slowly and calmly by Rowlands. Her trachea and oesophagus, jugular veins and carotid arteries had been torn, she would have bled out quickly, however he wasn't sure at this point whether this would have been the first wound, inflicted on this poor girl. He added that he hoped it was, as the alternative didn't bear thinking about. Her abdomen was open and exposed, from her sternum, virtually to her pubic area, a whole mess, as far as Huws could see, of guts torn and trailing.

Rowlands was by now working slowly and silently and minutes seemed to pass before he spoke again. Everything he said was recorded by the speaker over the table, not just for the purpose of the viewers behind the glass door, but to be kept on record and one day be submitted as evidence in court.

'DI, would you please come through for a few moments, you need to see this at closer quarters I'm afraid. Jane here will get you some PPE.' Pausing now, and turning his back to the table, as if relieving himself of the sight in front of him for a few seconds. His eyes shut.

Within seconds Huws was silently looking at the absolute total mess in front of him, the only part of the poor girl that was unmarked, was indeed her face and lower legs. The rest of her was either torn, disembowelled or deeply lacerated. The injuries were deep and dirty, filled with debris, soil and gravel from where she was found.

'I hope her neck wound was the first she suffered,' said Rowlands. 'Believe me, in all my years of pathology, this is like nothing I've ever seen before, totally barbaric and inhumane. Carried out I would say by someone in an utter frenzy.'

Silence. Neither of them knew quite what to say or do for the moment, stunned. Rowlands had put down his scalpel and was busying himself trying to tidy up the scene in front of him. Normally the bodily organs would have been weighed and replaced, however there were none to weigh, her liver, spleen and stomach had gone. Her chest cavity had not been penetrated, but any remaining intestines were carefully replaced back in the abdominal cavity, and Rowlands placed a thin layer of plastic over her before replacing a clean sheet over the body. Huws believed, at that moment in time, that the image would forever be etched in his brain and would surely be the visions of future nightmares.

He followed Rowlands out of the room, after he and Jane had slid the poor girl's body into one of the many fridges in the adjoining room. What tales could that girls spirit tell? He sat down in Rowlands office; Rowlands had his head in his hands, not a word passed his lips for what seemed many minutes.

He opened a drawer in his desk, bought out a bottle of Whisky and three glasses. One each for himself and Huws, and one for his assistant Jane, who had stayed behind to wash down the autopsy area. She would join them shortly.

'Sorry, I can't drink on duty,' said Huws looking longingly at the glass of whisky being poured.

'Take it,' said Rowlands, 'we all need it.' He didn't resist for long. He held it in his hands for barely a few seconds, then downed it all in one, followed by a hasty retreat to the nearby lavatory.

'That was a waste of bloody good whisky,' muttered Rowlands as Huws returned to his seat, mopping his sweaty brow with his hanky. Another glass was waiting for him on the desk. 'Keep that one down, it's good stuff, too good to waste.'

Jane joined them, having removed her coveralls and took a chair in the corner. She had clearly been crying. Having done this job almost from leaving school, she was normally a tough nut, but this was totally beyond anything that had gone before. The fact that her long- time colleague had simply gone to the office and sat down, was telling. Normally he would have helped with the clean-up, whistling while he worked, making the odd dry joke, as was per usual amongst people who worked amongst the dead, day in day out. Never at the expense of the deceased, or at least very rarely, just general banter, so that they went home after having enjoyed a bit of a laugh. People outside of these occupations rarely understood it, thinking them hard and a tad offensive.

Chapter Eight

THE MEETING WAS CALLED for 8 a.m., DI Huws taking charge. He had to admit to being a tad apprehensive, this was likely the biggest job of his career. He wouldn't call the area a backwater, but other than the nagging wife case, the Nettletons, before his time and the odd burglary, he was lucky to cover a relatively peaceful part of this corner of Wales. It would more than likely be his last big job before his retirement in a couple of years' time too.

Anyway, he needed to get his team briefed, and the post mortem photos that he had in the A4 envelope would no doubt be pinned onto the wall, in the room which had been requisitioned in the local community centre as their base during the case, the local police station did not have a big enough room. Huws also preferred to work in the community where the incident happened, it often gleaned more information.

The officers, however work hardened, would be shocked to see the pictures. He passed the brown envelope to his detective sergeant, who pulled them out and walked to the wall without looking at the pictures. He singled the first one out and tucked the others under his arm as he reached up for the pins. This bought the photo right to his eyeline, Huws was convinced he heard a gasp as he dropped the main pile on the floor and just pinned the first onto the wall.

'Come on now Howard, get on with it lad'. said Huws, knowing the poor man was clearly shocked.

The photos were pinned up one by one in all their gruesome horror and one by one the team stopped talking as their eyes fell on the photos. Howard stood dumbstruck, a couple of steps back from the wall. Huws let them have a minute to absorb what they were seeing. He felt for them, some were still relatively young, certainly they would not have seen anything like this before. He himself had gone home and hugged his teenage daughter last night, much to her surprise as they had never been a family that hugged each other for no particular reason, in fact his daughter seemed to think that he and his wife were the worst parents ever, at the moment, but that was just adolescence, he remembered being much the same at the her age.

'Right, I think we can all see what we have here, it's unbelievable what we saw yesterday, and we need to get to the bottom of this as quickly as possible. Whoever was capable of doing this is extremely dangerous and needs to be caught, before this can happen again, so come on, where do we start?'

'Fingerprints?' said a young PC drafted in to do some of the basic leg work on the case, as were a few others.

'There were no fingerprints,' said Huws, 'No obvious footprints at the scene either, though they are still looking. The area is loose soil and grit and had clearly been disturbed but so far not a shoe print or any other trace of anyone having walked down there that day, other than the old guy who found her.' He paused, not convinced the team were totally listening, they were still staring at the photos. 'Cause of death cannot be exact as yet, other than the actual injuries would have caused her to bleed out very quickly. The hope is that the first attack was maybe from behind to the neck, so that she may have been dead before her disembowelment, I can only hope. This was clearly a frenzied attack by some nutcase who once he started, totally lost it. He paused for effect, to allow the full enormity of what they were dealing with to sink in. Her liver and spleen have been removed and have not been found as yet. There is a fingertip search going on as we speak, but clearly, it's difficult taking into account the terrain.'

'There is no physical evidence of sexual assault, in fact she was fully clothed from the waist down. As you can see, she was eviscerated, the contents of her abdomen were not surgically removed but torn out, her trousers and panties were still on. Forensics are still doing further tests, they will obviously check for semen internally and externally, but so far, no fibres, hairs or any evidence has been found which could have been deposited by the killer, her shirt has been ripped to shreds.

Whoever has done this has certainly covered their tracks. There is an inkling in the higher echelons that it could be some sort of act of black magic, but there is nothing solid to confirm that either at this point in time.

'Sir, do we have any idea regarding the weapon?' asked a young WPC who was busy taking notes.

'No, we don't. As I said, none of the wounds were incised, they were torn, lacerated I think was the term used, whatever instrument has been used, at the moment, I just cannot imagine.'

'We need to get out there now and ask some questions, house to house, every single property in the area before whatever nut job has done this gets away, though more than likely they have legged it anyway. Remember, holiday cottage changeover day is upon us soon, so if a bunch of you can concentrate on any addresses we have locally and cover them first, that might help. If someone has seen or heard anything strange or someone acting suspiciously. There are a couple of cottage agents around locally, Beaumaris or Menai Bridge, see if they can help you with a list of addresses, and maybe even names of anyone who may have been on a short break for a few days, or any properties which have been vacated early. Rest of you get in amongst the locals, it will be everywhere by now anyway, you know what the jungle drums are like hereabouts.'

He looked around the room, normally people would be bustling about now getting on with various tasks or chasing leads to follow.

Today there was a sombre silence, stunned, he thought. 'Go on then, get on with it.'

Chairs scraped the floor as people got up, papers shuffling, laptops shut down by some, switched on by others, searching no doubt for contact numbers of various parties. A couple paused to look closer at the photos as they passed.

'Howard, you get down to the forest see if SOCO have come up with anything new.'

'Yes Sir.'

Policing had changed since he started, as a cadet, he was married to the job, hence his late marriage and entry into the world of fatherhood. He had been mentored through the ranks, and because he was single, had not been granted a police house, but lived in a variety of digs in whichever village he had been posted to, and they were quite a few. Mainly rural stations. Most villages having a police house and a local bobby on the beat who knew his patch, and every single person on it good and bad.

Most jobs had been petty burglaries, a few speeding fines, always a local willing to grass on others, to seek favour for whatever wrong doing they may have been involved in themselves.

His era had started at the very end of the hippy era, there were loads of them dotted around this area having moved into semi derelict cottages on hillsides that the locals looked at in disdain, in favour of their seventies housing estates, many built by local cowboy builders cashing in on the sixties baby boom and the need for housing. Most of these hippies were mature people now, carving livings for themselves in a whole variety of ways. Some had lost their homes in the early to mid-seventies to language nationalists who set incendiary bombs off in their houses, particularly if they thought they were holiday homes in the effort to keep the area Welsh.

Welsh was, and still was the local language despite their claims it would die out, the primary schools were Welsh, and most incomers integrated well, making great efforts to learn the lingo. Many of the activists were now also mature in age and attitude. Policing was very much at local level with larger town stations and then the HQ for the area in Caernarfon.

Policing was very much more distant now, he didn't know some of his colleagues further afield, times had certainly changed. Some of the team sent here now for this job, he was not familiar with, but no doubt that would change over the next few days. Hopefully not weeks or months.

Chapter Nine

MIKE AND STEVE paddled quietly around the headland. It was a glorious day, sunshine and just the hint of a breeze, barely tangible. An ideal day for it. They had driven with their wives to Penmon point, and been dropped off with their kayaks, and whilst the ladies had gone for a coffee in the old white cottage which now served as a café, they got their togs on ready to launch. Wet suits and light-weight anorak and buoyancy aids on, and mobiles in their water-proof pouches. Plans for the day had been made.

A paddle around the headland to Llanddona Bay where their cars and respective wives would be waiting for them, no doubt after a bit of retail therapy in Beaumaris on the way through. They both enjoyed their jaunts on their sit on kayaks, preferring them these days to the sit in variety they once had, capsizing and trying to get out now at their ages was not as easy as it used to be. They used to fish for mackerel in the past and virtually fill their kayak to almost sinking point with fish. Those days were long gone. Now in their early seventies just being able to get from A to B safely was an achievement.

The view from the perspective of the sea around this headland was always a pleasure, shingle beaches at Penmon giving way to steeper cliffs and rock shelves, old quarry workings and narrow rock clefts, before an expanse of the golden sands of Llanddona beach, which just blended on at its western end to the popular Red Wharf Bay.

There was a fair depth of water under them here, but it was clear and blue and today sparkling in the sunlight, necessitating the use of sunglasses against the glare. Steve wished he had used some sun screen, being fair skinned he would no doubt look like a lobster tonight. He had refused the offer from Kate when they parked, however, as always, she'd been right as she tended to remind him at every opportunity.

Getting around the first corner from the steep shingle beach at Penmon itself was the only challenging part of the paddle, where the swell could still be left over from the tide racing through the Sound between the mainland and Puffin island. Once around the corner it would be fairly leisurely. They passed the huge fish farm, a blot from the sea but thankfully well hidden from the landward side, with the coastal path diverted well away from it. Many locals did not even know it was there. On, past Shore house - a lonely cottage all set back off the edge. Mike had always wondered about its history, it was a fair way down from the track off the lane at Caim too, he presumed it was a holiday cottage now like many others in the area.

The paddle from Shore house to their first break point at White beach was a fair distance for two old boys, but there was no rush at all on a day like this, so on they went.

White beach, or Traeth Gwyn to give it it's Welsh name. A beautifully hidden shingle cove, popular with local fishermen for its seasonal Mackerel, Whitebait and Bass, but also the curse of the amateur, where fishing off the rocky slabs meant tackle lost numerous times as it gets caught in the rocky depths. With the chance of the odd seal virtually stealing the catch as it was reeled in, so best results were often achieved at low tide.

The small bay had once housed a quarry and jetty, blown up in the seventies. The remains of an old water tank were still at the top, where the road to the headland ended, leading onto Fedw Fawr, an area of local natural beauty.

Most tourists to the area completely missed out on White beach, it was not waymarked at the top of the road and being single track for a fair distance, many town dwellers were simply scared of venturing down the road, for fear of needing to reverse, which city folk seemed totally incapable of.

They reached the shore and pulled both kayaks up the shingle. The beach was empty. Ten minutes were spent stretching stiffening legs, and just generally enjoying the silence. For whatever reason there weren't many birds about today.

On they went beyond Fedw Fawr, heading now towards the next stretch of shingle, which was the area known as Carreg Onnen, another quarry long abandoned. A few cottages were above on the headland, accessed by a track which had suffered a landslip and become impassable a few years before, and the hamlet of Pentre Llwyn which had housed a few quarry workers, as had many of the cottages in the village of Llanddona up atop the hill.

Neither had ever paddled into this Bay.

'Shall we pull in here and have a look around?' said Mike.

'Yeah, go on then, we've time. The girls won't be back for another hour at least and it's a nice day,' answered Steve.

It was a rocky shore similar to White beach, large and small pebbles rounded off by centuries of waves. The slope up this beach however was far steeper than White beach, creating difficulties for by now fatigued legs, as they made their way up the stone ridges. They took care to pull their kayaks well out of the water, in case they simply slid backwards into the sea. Many stones here had holes right through and the occasional fossil to be found.

They made their way closer to the cliff face. Quarry work ended many years ago, and there were remains of just a couple of buildings. There was the usual evidence however of human spoil, the ring of stones created as a firewall for a makeshift barbeque, remnants of charred sticks and what Mike particularly hated, rusting empty beer cans.

'Why the hell don't people just take out what they bring in?' he muttered.

'Sheer laziness and lack of respect for the environment probably,' answered Steve. 'It doesn't half stink around here though, I shan't be staying long, must be a dead sheep around somewhere.'

'Hmm,' said Mike, 'or a seal.'

Whether it was because it was unfamiliar territory, or because of the stench they decided to move on.

'Hang on for a minute' said Mike, 'I need a pee.' Off he disappeared to the left of the big roofless brick shed towards the lee of the cliff, probably a dynamite store or similar when the quarry was productive.

'Jesus Christ Almighty,' shouted Mike as he reappeared, 'There's a rotting body here, behind the shed, not much left of it, bones picked dry by carrion I should think, we need to phone the police.'

'Bloody hell, are you sure? Is it not maybe the remains of a seal or porpoise?' said Steve.

'I've never seen a seal wearing trainers, have you? Have you still got that App you showed me on your phone, to be able to give the police a grid reference

Chapter Ten

'RIGHT LADS, it's Explorer 263 and grid reference 583 821,' said D I Huws, 'Any of you lads or ladies' experts in map reading? I'm going to pass the details on to the Coastguard, but we need to see where we can get the nearest access point. A decomposed body has been found on a beach somewhere around Penmon. We need to close it off and stop any public getting there.'

'That shouldn't be a problem Sir,' said a voice from the back of the room, Detective Sergeant Pete Smith, a keen hill walker was already on to it on his computer. 'There is very little chance we will get there other than on foot, the nearest cottage by track is Bodola and from then on its just marked as a path, not even a public one. More than likely just an old quarryman's path, so it may well be impassable, there's also been a landslide between the lane and Bodola track so we will need to walk in, unless we can be taken by sea?'

Two hours later, after a lot of organising, Huws was overseeing the RNLI crew and Coastguard volunteers bagging the deceased. They'd had to organise two trips from Beaumaris to bring SOCO to the scene.

All relevant photos had been taken, and it seemed a bit daft to keep the scene as found for any longer than needed today, they could get on with the post mortem and he could get a team here first thing in the morning, to look around for any other evidence. He was quite certain that there had not been anyone at the scene or it would most certainly have been reported. Being off the beaten track and barely accessible he was quite happy in himself to release the body, and the two gents who had found it.

Steve and Mike were to be taken back to Beaumaris in the lifeboat, the crew carefully secured their Kayaks across the stern. They both sat motorbike style behind the helmsman, certainly a quicker way back. It would have been quite exhilarating had it just been for any other reason.

The boat trailer was already in the water, waiting to re house the boat, masses of people watching and taking photos, totally oblivious no doubt of what had been developing, not two miles away or so as the crow flies. Marian and Kate were already there, Steve having phoned them from the beach, without telling them the full story but emphasising that they were both just fine.

The scenes of crime officers had not been long deciding that there was little to be found at the location of the body, no evidence of anyone else having been involved, no footprints to be seen or any tyre tracks anywhere near the top of the quarry, other than tractor tracks belonging to the neighbouring landowner. He had no cause whatsoever to make his way down the track to the quarry as it wasn't part of his tenancy. Within a few hours the scene looked as if no one had set foot there ever.

Huws walked up the slope from the beach, blowing, he couldn't actually walk and talk with the SOC officer who accompanied him. He made a note to make more effort with his level of fitness or at least lay off the pies and pastries which were always an all to convenient snack during the day.

He had parked his car at the nearest point to the path, a pull in on a bend near the base of an old hill fort, apparently occupied prior to the Roman invasion. On a rare day off, he had walked to its flat top with the dog, you could see right enough why this would have been chosen for its all-around view. As far as the Isle of Man on a haze free day, towards the west of the island and clear views towards the mainland of Gwynedd with fantastic views of the Snowdonia hills.

He changed from his wellies to his shoes, wellies had not been the best choice for the terrain, lacking grip on loose slopes, he chucked them in the boot before phoning Jane at the Pathology department.

'Another one incoming,' he said.

'Already here,' she answered. 'Prof. will have a look at it first thing in the morning. Is there anything we need to know about it?' she asked.

'Nothing specific really, I'm assuming it is likely a missing person, though as yet the team haven't linked it to anyone local, however it's obviously early days, they have only just been told about it in the last hour. They will extend the net over the next couple of days to other force areas. I don't for a minute think there is anything suspicious about it, some poor sod has more than likely come down here to spend his last few hours.'

Eight a.m. coffee in hand, not the nicest either, why couldn't the average machine just produce normal boring coffee like he made at home? He needed to reduce the amount of caffeine he drank anyway, having had a couple of episodes of palpitations that his Dr had put down to too much caffeine.

He made his way towards the mortuary, the hospital had expanded hugely since it was first built in the eighties, replacing the original small hospital, which stood on a site now housing a super-market in the student area of the city. Unbelievable that it could actually have functioned at its size, but then again it had many satellite hospitals around the North West that people were transferred, to when the acute illness had improved, or more morbidly where they were sent to die, nearer home, and visiting family.

Most of these had shut now due to government cuts, so the current edifice on the hill was always full to overflowing. God help anyone needing an ambulance in a rush these days. The counties ambulances and crews were often stuck for hours, outside the casualty department for lack of space upstairs in the wards. He hoped every time he came here that he would have no need for it himself any time soon.

Jane was waiting for him, Rowlands already prepared and gloved. A quick nod of acknowledgement as he drew back the sheet. The remains were already stripped of the clothing remnants and footwear, bagged by officers at the scene for investigation.

'Mm,' mumbled Rowlands, 'Male, around one eight five centimetres.' He glanced at Huws, 'That's six-feet to you and me, though I can be a bit more accurate when we have done measurements. Jane, can you get on with that please?'

This type of autopsy was not an everyday occurrence for Rowlands, and he didn't quite follow the same procedure as his otherwise daily methods. He would usually have started with a large Y incision to reveal the internal organs, which would have been carefully examined in situ before removal and weighing pre dissection. This poor sod was basically a collection of bones, barely held together with rope-like remnants of ligaments, all tendons, softer muscle and fat long gone. There wasn't even a single maggot anywhere, an empty skull devoured via the eye sockets.

Jane continued with her camera work, concentrating on the skull and its tombstone teeth discoloured by sun exposure. Huws was thankful at least that most of the teeth were there, providing a chance of some dental record identification. He continued to watch through his glass screen but needed to stand and move his position for a better view, when both Jane and Rowlands seemed deep in conversation closely studying the thigh bone of the right leg. He pushed the communication button, cleared his throat.

'Anything interesting I should know about?'

'Well, mm, we are seeing some striated marks on the femur bone, but more likely to have happened post mortem, strange really as the carrion you would expect would be birds, foxes and maybe badgers, but I do know there aren't that many badgers in this immediate area. Could be dog tooth marks, is it an area where you would get many dogs?'

'No, I wouldn't think so, it's off any public footpath,' said Huws.

'Ok, likely a fox has had a good gnaw at it too. It's difficult to give a date of death in this case, let alone a time of death with the bones having been bleached clean, and virtually every scrap of flesh stripped off. There are a few tests we can do to try to both age the remains and give an estimation of how long that the poor bugger had been there. The fact it was outdoors, exposed to the elements as opposed to buried, is slightly more difficult because some of the tests that are done include histological examination, and reactions between amino acids, degradation of Lipids and so on. Obviously modern Forensic DNA profiling, radio isotopic and radiological techniques will give us a bit more info,'

Huws tried to look as if he understood most of what he was being told, but the minutiae of pathology speak was generally beyond his comprehension. 'What I can tell you however is that whoever this is suffered a fracture of the left femur at some point in their life , probably in the last five years, and has had at least three of his ribs on the same side broken, so maybe a sporting injury, or involvement in a car crash. His teeth looked to have been healthy, with just one amalgam filling in his number 29 tooth lower right.'

Huws nodded, a little bit to go on for his team to go through the national missing persons list to see if that threw up any clues.

'The results for his age won't take too long, but the length of time he has been there may take a little longer, but in my humble estimation it may well be a year, maybe even a couple of years, so no point looking for a recently missing person.'

Huws mumbled a thank you as he made to leave, no post P.M. whisky this time.

Chapter Eleven

LIFE CHANGED SLIGHTLY from that day in the village of Allt Goch, as reverberations of the shocking discovery spread far and wide over the island. Despite it being two hundred and seventy- five squared miles with a rough population of seventy thousand, it was said to be the largest village in Wales, despite its many towns and villages.

It was a community, particularly for the original inhabitants who had been born there and everyone knew each other despite maybe living twenty miles apart. Soon there was gossip and speculation about the possible murderer living amongst them. The police were even receiving regular calls from people declaring that they had a 'strangely behaving neighbour'.

Nothing yet had been forthcoming from the missing persons list, and the net of search was spreading beyond the localised area for possibles. That, Idris Huws feared was going to take time. There had been a press release with some details given, it had to be done to stop the local press hounding them. It was one of the things he hated now, social media, never an issue when he first joined. You always had a couple of local reporters who you got to know, and largely they reported, to help police not thwart their investigations.

Now there was Facebook, Twitter. He should know, his daughter's face was glued to her phone screen every chance she got, talk of likes and shares. Unfortunately, it also caused the police problems, due to the fact that, the local papers posted on their pages, people were able to leave comments, sometimes hundreds of them, causing pain and upset to many families.

One of the things he warned his team about constantly, was not to give the papers any information whatsoever referring to anything sensitive, until the next of kin were notified. Another aspect that wasted manpower on scene now, was having to delegate someone simply to be aware of people taking photos and videos at scenes of accidents, and then immediately putting them onto these various social media platforms. He thought it horrific that next of kin were finding out about the death of relatives via a post online.

Times had changed, he doubted it would go back to as it was. He was however quite glad that he was the only I.T. dinosaur in his team, as the technology they now had available at their fingertips was way beyond him. He seemed to remember that in his last year at secondary school the library room was being re organised to allow for the introduction of word processors, words such as floppy discs and hard drives being bandied about were way into the future, word processors, if his memory served him right, were just glorified electric typewriters. He wondered if there would be a day when his inability to understand, or in fact refuse to put his mind to it, would mean him not being able to do his job.

Chapter Twelve

SUMMER DAYS SHORTENED INTO AUTUMN, the dominant earthy smells of plants receding into the earth, dropping leaves and hunkering down for the winter, filled the air. Decaying leaves on the ground produced a musky sweet smell. The long days of summer behind now, visitor numbers definitely reducing in Beaumaris, the local town. Blackberry visitors, as his mother used to call them. That saying, had as a child led to a belief, that they visited in order to collect the succulent autumn blackberries, and not the actual time of year when they were ripe. Silverheads, was another description, older people, coach tours making the most of the fact that children had gone back to school and places were generally quiet.

On a miserable rainy day, you could pop to the shop and see no one, a big difference from the hustle and bustle of summer. The real outdoor enthusiasts enjoyed this short autumnal window before winter set in, to walk the coastal path and visit locations which would previously have been too busy. Anglesey was glorious in good weather, it seemed to have pockets of micro climates, you could always find a place having sunshine whilst others had rain.

In winter it could take on a different identity, ferocious westerlies or easterlies raging across the landscape. Many hedgerow saplings doubled over at ninety degrees from the prevailing winds, unable to grow straight under its power. There are a few coniferous forests dotted around the island, wind blow being an issue with these as well, many of them now under the control of conservation bodies, who no longer managed them for wood production, in the name of protecting some animal species or other.

Instead, many which had been previously inaccessible to the general public had footpaths woven through them for walkers, cyclists and horse riders. Country parks had opened and old mine workings on the east of the island had paths created for walkers and mountain bikers. The sea was also now a playground not just for the rich and wealthy jet ski summer noisy invaders, but centres teaching safe kayaking, paddle boarding and coasteering, and such like. It was not surprising therefore, that the population more than quadrupled in a normal year, many a farm outbuilding, converted into bunkhouses and self- catering units, creating extra income to make up for ever reducing income from farming.

Philip Morrison raised his hood further over his head, pulling the elastic drawstring shorter. He had set off through the forestry on Mynydd Llwydiarth in bright sunshine and blue skies, but the rain had soon set in and seemed to be settled to stay for the whole day. The hills of Snowdonia were sending over a share of heavy rain. The tree tops towering above him, looked like millions of cathedral spires doing a seductive swaying dance, like a thousand witches' brooms, reaching for the skies.

The main track through the forestry would take him out to the main road, towards the village of Pentraeth, but he had no plans to go that far today, just a general meander through the woods, which were still relatively unfamiliar to him. He had only moved into the area a few months ago.

His wife Mary, had recently died, after a long battle with an inoperable cancerous brain tumour. He hadn't made many new friends in the village yet. They had started the purchase of their new house before she got poorly, and subsequently diagnosed. He had wanted to defer the move, so as not to cause her anymore anxiety than needed, while she was having what turned out to be futile treatment. She was having none of it, she pushed him to proceed and they duly moved. In fact, it worked out well, in the last few weeks, the most dedicated palliative care team stepped in from the local hospital trust, and with the aid of the most fabulous Macmillan nurse towards the end, Mary had the death she wanted, if there is such a thing. Once she knew that there was no more treatment and that she was terminal, she planned everything, taking everything out of his hands, knowing he would unlikely be able to cope by himself.

There were no children to worry about, that was a choice they had made when they got married 28 years previously. Their parents were both alive then, and although nothing was said, it was clear that they were considered selfish, to not produce grandchildren to be doted over. Neither of them was particularly child minded, they enjoyed their time together, their activity filled holidays at home and abroad. They compared this freedom with some of their friend's lives, who seemed to have lost their own, but had melted into a routine of doing things, which mainly pleased the children. Maybe they themselves were selfish, but it was their choice at the end of the day.

Now the love of his life, and very best friend was gone. Life, had changed for him when she went, the aftermath of Mary's death had been a blur of organising death certificates, sorting out bank details from joint accounts to just his, and the funeral which was a green burial in a willow basket casket. Neither of them were religious, so friends had been asked to say a few words at the simple ceremony. It had been held on the mainland in one of the few places allowed to do non-religious ceremonies. He had been unsure of the location initially, but was persuaded by Mary that there was no need for him to make a weekly pilgrimage, to visit the graveside which would in fact be a newly planted sapling, to draw on her decaying body as fertiliser, and he was, she had told him, under no circumstances to buy flowers, which were very expensive and would simply rot.

This was Mary to the core, realistic and simple. She had told him that her spirit would be with him everywhere he went, and that he was to try his best to find himself another partner, as he would certainly starve to death or eat rubbish without her there. They had these conversations in the last few weeks of her life, and although they found they could laugh at her ideas at the time, the reality of it had left him a totally broken man.

Life had changed, he had changed, local people had initially made an attempt to make friends and invite him into their community, but everything he had done before had been with Mary. He wasn't one for Choir singing, book clubs or anything like that, he walked, and walked, and walked. He was a web builder by trade, and since Mary's death, his days had no routine, no timetable, no normality. He got up late, normally after a sleepless night, skipped breakfast or ate an inevitably overripe banana, the healthy diet produced for him by Mary now a long- gone memory, his appetite had seemingly died along with his wife. He walked the coastline and local area, returning home at dusk, to then sit until the early hours dealing with work e-mails and design requests. He appreciated, it must be frustrating for clients that he didn't respond to mail, until they had likely been asleep for hours. No doubt he had lost clients by his erratic business patterns. He didn't particularly care.

Friends had drifted away, he had become unsociable, choosing not to use social media, looking at the caller's name on his mobile phone, often choosing not to answer, dependent on how he felt at that precise moment. He was fed up to the back teeth of people asking how he was doing. Initially he would just nod and mumble an ok, but in all honesty, he felt like screaming at them, 'How the hell do you think I feel? I've lost the only person in the world I well and truly loved, I feel like shit, all the time, every hour, every day,' but he never did. It was not their fault.

He walked on along the gravelled track, there were two properties that he had seen in this forest as far as he could tell, one which had some pretty ferocious dogs running outside, and thankfully a sturdy looking gate. He'd not actually seen anyone there, so he was unsure of the property status. The rain was increasing now, so instead of continuing along the track he decided to turn off to his left, seeing a well- trodden path veer off amongst the trees. Pine cones and newly fallen needles littered the ground, which was firm underneath his feet, no bogs here like lower down towards the beach. Trees creaked and groaned around him straining against the wind, whipping and weaving through the trunks, some having already succumbed and fallen, causing him to have to scramble over the odd one and duck under others. One tree was totally devoid of bark, virtually hollowed out, it looked like a discarded wasp nest, so damaged was it, from years of endless drilling by a woodpecker. It had clearly been determined.

Remains of ancient moss-covered stone walls occasionally crossed the path, the remnants no doubt of smallholding boundaries of long ago, long abandoned when a rich landowner was made an offer, they couldn't refuse by the forestry commission. He and Mary had both hated the forestation of hills, after a trip to the highlands of Scotland one January, where they saw dozens of dead deer, just above a forestry fence line. They had not been able to get through to lower ground for food or water, clearly all the streams up high had been frozen. He remembered there had been uproar about it at the time, apparently this was no longer allowed to happen. Recent visits had been more pleasing, they had seen large herds of deer on lower ground below the forests, some herds even wandering the village streets in some of the more remote west coast corners. How they loved those holidays. It was strange that to one person, deer could be a means to financial benefits, and to others a cause of misery as they ate everyone's vegetable plots. They couldn't win either way.

This was how his brain worked now, random thoughts popping into his head, taking him off on tangents all over the place, it affected his work too. On one hand he despaired, on another he didn't care. He didn't care now what anyone thought of him. The area up ahead seemed to brighten up a little, more sky showing through, a clearing so he pushed on. Suddenly ahead, as if dropped there, a chimney stack rose out of the ruinous bed of concrete and bricks, the remains of a house? Was this maybe the old local estate's summer residence that he had heard of? Certainly not much of it left now, a brick- built gable with a long empty fireplace stood at the opposing side, random ironwork and decayed sheets of tin.

Glancing left through the bramble covered undergrowth he saw a glimpse of open water. Clearly this was the boathouse spoken of. On closer inspection, it may have been in its time a substantially sized lake, but now bulrushes and reed beds stretched out into the water, reducing its surface area. Ducks swam gracefully away from his direction, surprised no doubt at having their peace disturbed. A single swan could be seen in the distance, possibly a mate would be sheltering on a reed nest somewhere. There was no defined path around the lake that he could see, not unless he wanted to get his feet wetter than they already were.

He stepped back towards the concrete chalet base, put down his small backpack and took out his water container. The wind still hooleyed around him, he felt that the rain was not quite as bad now, or else he was largely protected by the tree canopy overhead. Other than the wind there was no other sound to be heard. Too far from the road for traffic, not enough birdlife other than the odd quack and the sound of beating wings against water, as one either landed or took off. He heard an occasional crackle of twigs around him, more than likely rabbits in the undergrowth scuttling about their daily business, or maybe a fox.

There were supposedly lots of Red squirrels in this particular wood, initially part of a local release programme, but now apparently doing well, though he had never caught sight of one, possibly because walking along staring at your feet, deep in thought did not make the best of what was around him. He had, he thought seen a couple of feeder boxes on a couple of trees not long after he left the track. Someone must be monitoring them. The sky above the canopy was brightening now, blue with mackerel clouds, the pine tips not doing their swaying dance anymore, he pushed back his hood, and rubbed his dampened hair off his forehead. Just ahead was a rivulet, a crude bridge created across it by a fallen trunk. He knew that people came here with their mountain bikes, and actually created a few routes criss-crossing the forest, he had no issue with this, as they were at least quiet, compared to the moto- cross bikes, that seemed to enjoy cutting up the saltings, far below him on the edge of the beach that plagued the local residents, with their silencer- less exhaust noise and excessive revving. They did a fair bit of damage to the eco-system.

He stepped onto the log, damp with lichen and fungi, he almost lost his balance, suddenly all the air was forced out of him in a strangled gasp, something pushed him hard, sprawling scissor legged astride the log, his whole body involuntarily tensed against a heavy unrelenting weight. His face was pressed down into the stream bed, only literally an inch, no more, of sour pine needle filled water, but nevertheless filling his airways as he was grabbed tightly from behind around his neck. Please, please let me go, he thought, as his life blood ebbed away into the now dark crimson stream, running down to join the very lake he had just been admiring. Had he still been alive, he would have heard a loud cacophony of sounds, as all the birds in the surrounding area erupted out of the waters to escape.

Chapter Thirteen

DI HUWS CLEARED his throat for attention, after his entering the hall had not worked, all heads down, some on the phone, some typing away, one busy at a map of the UK sticking coloured pins in what at least appeared to be a purposeful fashion.

'Right, you lot, what do we have here, Unrhyw Lwc?' As he reverted to his native welsh language. 'Anyone had any luck with anything useful?' He looked around, as he put one bum cheek on the corner of the desk, where a young PC sat. He wondered if she had actually moved at all, since he had seen them last. She looked up at him.

'Well, the Missing persons bureaux has come up with five possibles for the description we have, we've already discounted three of them so far, but are still looking into the other two. We're in contact with next of kin, so hopefully we'll have some news on those by the end of the day.'

'Ok, good work,' he recognised the enthusiasm in her that he had as a young rookie, as soon as he had found his feet.

Policing was very different these days, and in his opinion, not always in a good way. Too many interferers higher up the social scale, too many do-gooder's believing in rehabilitation of offenders, when he knew all along that most of them were bad apples, despite any guidance they might be given. In his day a clip around the ear would have dealt with most minor offenders, but woe betide you doing that now. No, things had gone seriously astray in the judicial system, and sadly these young officers in this room would no doubt soon sour.

'Ok, so back to young Sarah, have we made any headway there at all? Any luck with the house to house visits?'

'No not really,' said a voice from the back of the room, 'Nothing to go on that had any solidity. A couple of cottage owners declaring their last guests as odd, but nothing more than 'not smiling back at them and being unsociable', though that particular lady, would no doubt have your life story off you in ten minutes given the opportunity.'

There would be very few people holidaying in the area at the moment who were single. This was still just about school holiday time, so families filled the streets and beaches.

'So, I take it no one has had any loners staying?'

'We still have a couple of cottage owners to catch up with, but they live away, and deal with the bookings themselves as opposed to using an agency. Mind you we did have a chat with a couple of local ladies who do the changeover cleaning too, though their main concern seemed to be the people who left the grill pan filthy, and left skid marks in the toilet bowl,' said Howard. 'These cleaning ladies however, rarely see the guests as they have left before they arrive to clean, and they in turn have gone before the next guests come in.'

'Thank you for your efforts so far, but we really need to get on with this now. Pressure is building up and time is of the essence. We have heard however that there is no evidence of sexual assault, so that doesn't look to be a motive, and I'm sure in a small way will be a relief to her parents. Whoever attacked her used something which was clearly not a sharp knife, but something which caused massive lacerations, tear wounds; a total nutter clearly. Also, at this point in time there is very little to link the two bodies, one clearly very recent, and the other we are awaiting tests, but clearly a fair time ago. Having said that though, let's not discount anything.'

He was desperate for a cigarette but had stopped a while ago. He walked out of the hall straight out onto the roadway outside. It was actually right next door to the village pub, but it was instilled into him as a young PC, not to ever go to the local pub. Apparently, he would lose respect in the community or so his seniors at the time drilled into him. Now, despite him actually not being in uniform for years, it was a habit he had never broken.

He pulled on his vape and strolled to his right towards the main village, releasing a cloud of white vapour in his trail, the road to his left wound its way steeply down a hill to the beach, and in fact a footpath off this hill would have led him to the now taped off scene of crime, which was still subject to a fingertip search. He shut his eyes and shook his head, still seeing the terrible scenes that had been in front of him, both at the scene and at the mortuary, he shook his head in despair, at the capabilities of someone to be sick enough in the head, to be able to carry out such an act.

Venturing as far as the bus stop, he noted it was decorated with bunting, not something he had seen before, maybe a village thing. A man was ambling slowly up the road, head down, clearly no intention of making eye contact.

'Diwrnod braf,' said Huws, more a question than a statement, hoping for an answer, this seemed to catch the man out, possibly not expecting a stranger in his village to speak Welsh, he hesitated, as he drew alongside on the other side of the road. 'Da chi yn byw yma?' asked Huws, simply asking if he was a local.

'Pwy sy'n gofyn?' 'Who is asking?' he replied.

Huws introduced himself, and crossed the road towards the man, whose face immediately took on a distinct look of suspicion or guilt, a look that sometimes appeared even if they had been paragons of virtue all their lives.

'I'm here with my team, investigating the tragic murder of a young lady, that took place the other day.'

'Yes, I know.' he mumbled quietly. 'You won't find the animal capable of doing that here in this village.'

'Possibly not, but we have to follow every avenue possible to bring this to the conclusion it deserves.' He slipped a card out of his wallet and passed it to the man. 'Do you have a name? It's good to get to know a few of the locals.' He immediately labelled the man standing in front of him as a quiet loner, and certainly not a criminal.

He seemed a little hesitant to divulge his name, but eventually mumbled, 'Iorwerth, Iorwerth Davies. Only an animal could do that to the poor girl,' he almost whispered, as he took the card out of his hand, stuffing it into his back pocket without even a glance.

Huws nodded in response, put his vape in his pocket, never as satisfying as the real thing, and no doubt a few years down the line it would be found to be as dangerous as the actual cigarettes. He walked back to the rear of the pub, where they had asked to park a few of the team cars, two young lads were sitting atop a picnic bench watching him.

'Do you know who killed Sarah yet?' asked the red head. 'Doing our best,' answered Huws. He needed to check on the forensics team at scene, and then visit the girl's parents to see if he could find anything more than his DS had already done.

Chapter Fourteen

JENNY TIED Bella's lead rein to the ring on the wall and reached down for a body brush and curry comb. She loved the horse's coats at this time of year, soft and silky with a natural shine provided by good grass and sunshine.

She couldn't remember a time when she didn't ride, or in fact live in the forestry. Not a single main road did she have to venture along if she chose not to, unless she took the track to the lane that led to the vast expanse of beach, that was locally called Red Wharf bay. The section of beach that she used, was called Wern y Wylan beach, after the little hamlet just up the hill. It wasn't that popular with holidaymakers, as the tide went so far out, it was a pain to walk out far enough to have sufficient depth to swim.

Many a happy afternoon she had spent here on young ponies and horses, exposing them to wide expanses of space, and paddling in the sea, jumping up and down banks on the salting's as well as the exhilarating gallops she had enjoyed. This was something she had educated herself about over the years, always walk the track you intend to gallop, in one direction just to double check that there were no tendon tearing soft patches, which would suck a horse's leg in up to the knees and catch out the unwary reckless rider. Many a horse had badly injured itself hereabouts.

Jenny took her time grooming, teasing out the ringlets in Bella's mane, always a nuisance with these Welsh Cobs, that tended to have a long thick mane, they twisted in the breeze, tails the same. This aspect of being with her horses gave Jenny just as much pleasure as the actual riding. She had a choice of a few to ride, having a father who had always taken an interest in breeding a few over the years, so most of the horses were related to each other, and were broken to ride when they reached the age for it. She knew the forest surrounding her home like the back of her hand, every path and dead- end track of it, every fallen log that she had used as a cross country fence when younger, though someone, and she suspected, it may be a local mountain bike enthusiast, had cleared some of these aside in recent years.

She lifted the saddle off the stable door next to her, placing it forwards on Bella's wither and gently sliding it back into position, pulling the saddlecloth up into the gullet of the pommel, so as not to create pressure. She grasped the girth from underneath and pulled hard to reach the straps with the buckle, it was always a competition between them, Bella blowing her tummy out as much as she could, in order for the girth to only just reach. At this point, Jenny would put on the bridle, gently lifting the metal bit up to Bella's tightly closed teeth, which always relented with the gentle insertion of a thumb into the corner of her mouth, and gentle pressure on her gums. It was never an argument between them, just a game Bella had always played.

By the time Jenny had stuffed her hair inside her riding helmet and released Bella from her knot on the wall, Bella would have forgotten to blow out her tummy, and Janet could do up the girth. It would need doing again once she had ridden a few hundred yards. She drew Bella alongside the step platform her father had built for her and her siblings many moons ago, though at that age she was able to gracefully vault onto her ponies. Not so nimble now. She grasped the reins in her left hand as she put her left toe in the near-side stirrup, reached over to the far side of the pommel and swung herself over, simultaneously finding the right stirrup. Bella was not the most patient of mares and took off as soon as Jenny's bum touched the saddle.

Yesterday's wind and rain had cleared, some trees could still be heard to creak in the breeze. Rarely were they totally still, but she loved the green tones speckling through the trees, more shades of green than she could even imagine there were names for. Bella swung along in her low ground covering stride, like being atop a big sofa, thought Jenny smiling to herself. She had her most interesting conversations when she was out riding, very one sided clearly, but her horses knew all her innermost secrets, hopes and wishes. They ambled on, reins in one hand, no contact with Bella's soft as velvet mouth, consequently she was able to plunge her head down and grab at some tall grasses alongside the track, creating a mass of green slather and spittle, that she would then spray all over Jenny, as she either snorted or flung her head to dislodge an imagined fly.

Jenny always used her time riding to daydream, making grand plans for her future, which actually wasn't very different from the life she currently lived in the forest now, with her ageing parents. She did worry a little about how her parents might cope with this location as they got older, but thankfully they were at present, fit and well albeit a little less active than they used to be.

She gently lay the right rein across Bella's neck, encouraging her to yield to the pressure, and move across off the gravel road onto a path. She liked this track, as the organisation which had taken on the responsibility of reintroducing the red squirrels into the forest, had feeders here and thereabouts on various trees. Perspex fronted peanut filled boxes with lids that the squirrel knew somehow to lift to access the nut supply. If she stood here quietly for a while, she regularly saw the beautiful russet coloured creatures go about their daily routines. It seemed that they were not in the least bit perturbed by the big lump of a horse being on their territory and seemed oblivious of the human perched atop. She would laugh to herself when the odd squirrel actually found the lid close above its head, whilst stuffing its cheeks with nuts, and for a few seconds would look pathetically out of the perspex before realising all it had to do was give a gentle upward push. She never managed to get her mobile phone out quickly enough, to get a really decent photo, before they were sprinting vertically up the trees into the canopy.

She reached the squirrel clearing but there seemed to be no one busy there today. She had learnt that the place to look was in fact way above her head in the tree canopy, they normally built their drays a fair way up, often in the branches of a fork in the trunk. There could be a whole motorway of activity going on above people's heads, when they came looking for these elusive creatures, but so busy were they looking at the feeders and the ground, they inevitably missed the activity above. She gave up today, shortened the reins a touch and gently squeezed her heels against Bella's side. There is nothing better than a Welsh Cob for picking its way along rough ground, a little bit like an all- terrain vehicle or four-wheel drive.

She knew this particular path was a dead end, but she loved seeing the remnants of the old farm walls, now toppled higgledy-piggledy and covered in a thick verdant moss, always damp and holding water regardless of how dry it had been. There had been five small farms on this hillside at one time, but theirs and next door were the only ones remaining, with another further along the hill towards Allt Goch, none of which were now farmed, it had almost been akin to the Highland Clearances when the present local lord's father had it all planted in the fifties. A couple of old ruined cottages could still be found if you knew where to look for them.

She could now smell the nearby lake, the slightly putrid scent of decaying waterside vegetation. The local gentry used to swim and fish in it apparently, many moons ago but in her lifetime and prob-ably longer it had just lain unused, unmanaged and reverting to nature, closing itself down at its edges to any chance of human recreation.

Belle tensed under her, her normally flabby fat covered muscles taking on a quiver all of their own. She stopped, and despite a nudge forwards by Jenny she rooted and stood her ground. She grew from her normal fifteen hands to seventeen, so much was the tension growing in every nerve of her body. She snorted, her ears pricked and rotated like a radar dish, listening out for whatever she clearly thought was out to get her. It was unlike Bella to do this, normally the most laid back and laziest of horses.

'Come on old girl,' said Jenny, a laugh in her tone. 'What's got you today.' Without warning Bella span her body around on her haunches, lowering herself, creating such a centrifugal force, that Jenny found herself slammed against the nearest tree trunk, which frightened Bella all the more, causing her to leap away leaving Jenny to fall heavily in the gap left between her shoulders and the tree. Jenny was thumped into the ground all the air pushed out of her body making her gasp like a dying fish, 'Oh Woah, woah,' she shouted, but Bella was showing her a clean pair of heels as she disappeared towards the way they came, stirrups flying, the heavy metal banging on her sides with every stride, and adding to her perceived fright ,at whatever she had imagined she had seen.

Jenny looked around for her glasses, or at least felt around, without them she couldn't see well enough to spot them. Thankfully they were just to the right of her, and better still undamaged. She had cut herself as there was blood on her hands. She wasn't too worried about Bella running off, there was no actual traffic to worry about, the two forest exits were gated, and she knew she would find her way home, though she cursed the long walk.

She wiped her hand on her jodhpurs and looked to see what damage she had done, inspected her hands but was surprised to find no cuts. She felt her face, thinking perhaps she'd had a nosebleed but no, nothing. Twisting around to see the backs of her legs. She saw that where she had hit the ground, there was blood on her clothing. It was only at this point that it occurred to her to look where she fell. Open mouthed and in disbelief, she saw that the ground near the tree was actually a dark crimson, soaked in puddle of blood, how could that have happened when she hadn't actually hurt herself?

There was no phone signal in the forest, so she knew trying to phone her dad to beg a lift was out of the question, so it was to be a long walk home, or they would see Bella by the gate without her and set off by car to look for her. It wasn't the first time in her life it had happened.

She made to set off, dusting herself down, assuming the scuff marks around her were from Bella's hooves and probably a fox that had clearly had a rabbit kill earlier. Being surrounded by foxes though she was quite surprised that Bella had reacted as she had. A thought struck her, what if the blood was Bella's, what if she had somehow hurt herself?

Suddenly a splash of colour caught her eye beyond the tree, it was a small backpack, the type she herself sometimes used if she walked along the beach and around the block. She leant down and picked it up. Looking around for a possible owner she opened the zip, feeling a bit like a thief, inside was a Mars Bar and small water bottle, the flask type that keeps water cold. There was also a rolled up lightweight rain coat.

Shouting out, 'Hello is there anyone around? Are you ok?' she listened for an answer, peering through the trees around her. A rain-drop fell landing on her cheek, she instinctively wiped it away. 'Oh my god.' she said to herself as she brushed at her cheek again and stared at her hand. 'Blood,' this time she looked up, and froze. 'Jesus Christ almighty,' she said, not that she was in the least bit religious.

High up above her head was a man seemingly hanging off a bough around twenty feet up and was clearly what Bella had seen or sensed. He appeared fully dressed but blood soaked. She couldn't see his face properly, she didn't want to, she was already jogging away along the path as fast as her legs could carry her, and she could get her breath.

She reached the gravel track, thank god downhill from here. She heard shouting 'Dad, dad,' almost not aware it was actually her screaming echoing back at her through the trees, no one answered, no one came, she ran, the last corner ahead of her now before she turned off the main track towards her home, she shouted again, this time her father's head appearing above the gate. Bella was there, no one had noticed her appearance.

'What the hell are you shouting at?' said Eric, seemingly not even aware that his daughter and her horse, had made their way home separately and under their own steam.

'Dad, there is a person hanging in a tree, not far from the lake. There is blood everywhere around the tree, I fell in it, Bella refused to go and span around dumping me over her shoulder.' All this was coming out like verbal diarrhoea, in between great gasps of breath and tears.

'Ok, ok, ok, calm down. Let's get this mare in and we will phone the police.'

'Listen, I will put her in, and untack her, you go in, you look like shit.' Eric was never one to mince his words, tough, ex forces, seen a few horrors in his time. Jenny went indoors, falling into the old dog's armchair in the kitchen, surprising her old mum Dot.

'Hi Love, you ok? You look as white as a sheet, are you not well, I thought you were out riding?' It all poured out like a river of panic, as the enormity of what she had seen hit her, alongside the bruising soreness that was now creeping up her right side as often happened after a fall, adrenaline coursing through a body initially, before it reduced and revealed the real intensity of pain. Her poor old mum stood open mouthed.

'Hung themselves, here? Poor soul, here let me just get you a cup of tea, your hands are shaking, poor love. How awful for you.' Eric stepped in through the door. 'Have you phoned the police?'

'No of course not yet, give us a chance, Jenny is very upset,' scolded Dot. Eric grabbed the hand's free phone off the sideboard and dialled 999. He explained to the police that he would need to drive to the Forest entrance to unlock the barrier for them, and that he would meet them there with Jenny who could then show them where the poor person was.

'Oh no dad, I don't want to go there again, I don't want to see it.'

'You won't need to look, but you can lead us down the path as close as you feel comfortable, come on, it won't take them long to get here from Llangefni, they said they would send someone straight away.'

He ushered Jenny to her feet and in a totally uncharacteristic move he hugged his daughter, Jenny wasn't sure if this almost shocked her as much as finding someone hanging from a tree. Eric ushered his daughter towards the car and went to open the gate. He was a battle-hardened man, and this sort of news from his daughter was in all honesty, water off a duck's back to him. Yes, some poor sod had felt the need to do this to himself for reasons known only to himself, but Eric was mainly concerned as always, with keeping his own family safe and secure, and would in all honesty go out of his way to protect them in any way he needed to. It was one of the reasons he had moved them to this place, many moons ago now and raised his children in its natural cocoon. The one thing that had given him a bit of a shake, was a purposely started forest fire in the early 90's, that had taken ten days to properly be extinguished. That had created a vulnerability that stupidly he hadn't planned for, but thankfully the culprit had been found and arrested.

Jenny sat in silence for the almost two- mile drive to the barrier, just glancing to her left as she passed the mouth of the path she had followed, shivering at the thought of the poor person hanging there. Why there? It would now forever be tainted with the vision of what she had seen, she would never be able go down that path again.

Eric opened the barrier, securing it back to the post then swung the car around in the entrance, to park and wait for the police. They sat in silence, he had never been good with all the tea and sympathy stuff, Dot had always been the one for that, he chose to just sit and stare, and lift his eyes to the rear-view mirror when a vehicle went past the entrance. On some days the entrance sides were filled with parked cars, usually people keen to catch a glimpse of the forest's elusive red squirrel colony. He had by now seen so many, the novelty had worn off. A car swung in behind him, a local panda car. He didn't waste his time getting out to acknowledge their presence, he simply raised his hand and drove on. They would know to follow.

'This path, next on the right?' he asked Jenny. She nodded. He pulled up the car, no effort to pull in, only they as a family regularly used the road, if the holiday home residents next door came along, they could damn well wait.

'I'm not coming,' said Jenny, 'you go, keep to the path, over the old field wall and it's a bit further than the little stream.'

'Ok, I will show them,' he answered as he did his coat zip up, his little effort to looking slightly tidier and more presentable.

'Don't forget you are not looking for it on the ground, the body was high up in a tree'. Jenny let out a sob again and closed her eyes as the vision of the poor person appeared in front of her. Eric strode off, followed by two uniformed policemen. She stared ahead, her whole environment somehow soured and spoilt. The sun was in the West at tree top level now, causing Jenny to squint as spears of sunlight broke through the now gently swaying treetops. What an awful thing to do to yourself on such a nice day she thought, contemplating what awful things must have happened to this person to do such a thing.

Suddenly, the door opened, and Eric slid back in beside her.

'I've been asked to leave the scene,' he said, 'Well, actually I've been asked to go and get a ladder for them. It's a man, but he isn't hanging, he's sort of wedged in a fork, they've sent for back-up.'

'Wow,' said Jenny, 'why would anyone be climbing the trees? Whatever he was doing he has clearly slipped, poor man, what a stupid thing to be doing.'

They set off along the track, a sudden thought occurred to Jenny, 'Is he actually dead? Oh Christ what if he isn't and I just went off and left him, that will be awful, I might have been able to help.'

'Don't be daft,' said Eric, 'How the hell were you supposed to actually get up the tree to do anything about it? The old mare probably smelt him, and then caught a glimpse of him above, you know what horses are like, their only instinct is to run, run first look later, you should know that by now.' He whistled out his breath between his teeth. 'Open the gate gal", he continued, Jenny's despair and upset to be forgotten. He raised them tough.

Chapter Fifteen

DI HUWS SAT in the store room that had been allocated to him as a makeshift office in the community centre. Mops and buckets and cleaning fluids moved aside, and the smallest table he had ever seen as a desk. He hadn't asked for an office, but had been ushered in here by Pritchard, who seemed determined to get him away from the rest of the team while they worked, probably because, by his own admission he could be a bit of a tyrant.

He had just come off the phone with Llangefni, a couple of uniform guys had just phoned from a forestry, a few miles east. A simple hanging is what they were expecting, but they apparently needed a team there now. They had got up to him, a local with a ladder had helped, but had immediately realised there was a fair bit more to it than first thought. The guy was indeed suspended up a tree, but seemingly there was no sign of hanging, he was wedged in a fork, and had been brutally attacked, his throat gaping open, and indeed could not be identified as his face was virtually torn away. Llangefni added that the two bobbies were in a bit of a state, and had in fact left the scene, they were now both sitting in the car on the main track, locked themselves in by all accounts.

He had told them to, 'Bloody well get back to the scene,' at which the reply was, 'Well, no one really goes down there anyway,' to which he reiterated, 'Well some people clearly do, as there is a guy up a tree without a face.'

Something didn't sit well with him about this, too many connections, similarities to the young girl maybe, and only a few days later. He didn't like it, he really didn't like what this was starting to look like. Two murders in almost as many days, and a skeleton, though he was reasonably happy that that find was a coincidence and likely an old suicide. He made contact with SOCO and they were on their way.

He entered the main office to tell them the news, but the young female PC butted in, 'I think we may know who the remains belong to. A 45-year-old male who went missing from Dyffryn near Barmouth in 2018, had a history of depression. Five foot eleven, his trainers match how he was dressed when he was last seen by his Mother. He told her he was going off into the hills to 'Get his head round stuff', something he did quite often. He had history for going walkabout without telling anyone where he was going, or how long for. He was wearing a shirt that matched the few torn remnants on his body, but she had no idea of the make at the time he was reported missing. She didn't report him missing for a week, because it's what he did. He refused to carry a mobile phone with him because he believed people were out to get him. He had however, taken his supply of medication; he was a registered schizophrenic. There was an extensive search for him following her eventually reporting him as missing. Our colleagues in that area have just confirmed that he was considered a vulnerable person, they had also involved a couple of their more local mountain and lowland rescue teams, concentrating mainly on the mainland in his local area. He was known to use busses and would hitch a lift. No searches were made for him at the time on Anglesey, but Mike is following up the CCTV footage from the Menai Bridge, to see if anyone matching his description had walked across. We're not holding our breath though because so many students from the University and the locals in general cross it every day, unless he crossed it at night, which makes spotting someone a bit easier, it's a bit of a needle in a haystack job. But they will see if they come up with anything.'

She had barely taken a breath whilst telling Huws this, all without looking at a single note. She was keen, fair play thought Huws.

'That's Great,' he said, now he could get a word in edgeways. 'Right, the team working on the scene of Sarah Jones's murder have finished there with nothing new to report, however I have just moved them on, not far away in fact, less than two miles. We had a young horse-rider who has come across a male victim of an attack, who somehow or other has been put up into a tree. We have absolutely no idea as yet how or why he was up there, but the first reports coming back are that he has been the victim of a vicious assault. Whoever has done this has clearly been in a frenzy, there are lots of similarities in the wounds inflicted I'm told.'

There was a sharp intake of breath to be heard around the room.

'Shit,' he heard one of the lads say. 'Is this connected to Sarah Jones do you think? It sounds as if the same instrument has been used.'

'We don't know yet, they are preparing to get him out of the tree at the moment, and secure the scene, we will know more when we get him to the pathologist.'

Chapter Sixteen

CAROLINE WAS JUST EMPTYING the contents of a pooper scooper into the wheelbarrow, when the yard phone rang. She walked to the feed room door where the phone was set up on the wall and answered.

'Hi,' is all she got out as the voice at the other end hissed down the line.

'There is a big cat in your bottom fields, get here now.' She had no idea who this was.

'Who is this, what did you say about a cat?' The voice hissed again, though a little more slowly.

'It's Tom, from along the beach, I'm on the bottom slope of my field on my tractor, topping, I'm able to see your water meadow at the bottom, there is a big cat in there, I've just seen it spray up a tree, It's huge. I'm whispering because I don't want it to see me. I don't want to attract attention to myself. I have no protection from it on this tractor, it hasn't got a cab. I've phoned the police before I phoned you, though I don't hold out much hope of them coming here any time soon. They wanted a grid reference and stuff, I don't tend to carry a map on my tractor. Do you have a shotgun?'

Caroline could only stare at the phone when Tom hung up abruptly.

'James,' she shouted as she ran past the barn and up the slope towards the cottage, 'James,' louder, she knew it was pretty pointless expecting him to appear promptly, he wasn't too good on his pins these days. She flung open the back door and there he stood, oblivious to her shouts, drying the dishes, clearly deaf too. 'Quick, we need to get down to the beach fields, Tom's just phoned from there and says there is a big cat in the field.'

'What colour?' asked James as if that really mattered.

'My god does it really matter? I didn't think to ask him, just go and get your shotgun out of the cabinet,' she said marching towards the car.

'Seems sad to shoot it", said James, as he turned towards the stairs to fetch his gun. He couldn't remember when he had last used it, as he stuffed some cartridges out of the box into his waistcoat pocket. He could hear the car outside the house now, Caroline no doubt purposely doing wheel spins up the gravel slope towards the cottage, and revving the engine meaning for him to hurry.

He hobbled down the stairs, he needed a new hip but with a history of a heart attack in ninety- four he wasn't keen to go under the knife. Lifting himself into the car, bum cheek at a time, and shuffling to face forwards, he shut the door and they were off down the track, gravel flying behind them.

Caroline paused at the drive entrance just to check there was no one coming off the beach to the left. The main road was a dead end at their entrance, theirs being the last property on this stretch of road, only the beach track opening out onto Red Wharf bay below the farm. The other properties were accessed from the Pentraeth side by a beach road, flooded at high tide. She drove the familiar twists and turns up the hill, knowing by instinct where she may meet another car. She could by now almost reverse as quickly as she could drive forwards, if needed. They reached the village, turned left and continued past the pub and down the Allt Goch hill towards the beach. She drove straight down to the field gate. Tom was there in his land rover waiting for her, as was Aled who lived just up the lane.

'Where is it now?' said Caroline.

'I lost sight of It,' Tom responded, looking around himself like a fully trained commando. Clearly anxious, and with reason. 'It went towards the bank of trees between your field and the beach café and little park area. I drove the tractor to the land rover and swapped, phoned Aled here for some moral support, he told me about the murder in the woods too, had you heard?'

'Good God no,' said James who had by now joined them. They both listened as Aled went through the news again.

'We haven't heard anything about this, and it's only up the road from us too, in fact, I walk through those woods fairly regularly with the dogs to check on the horses, saves driving all the way around when the tide is right in. That's awful, and here too, we never have things like this happening in this area.'

The discussion had almost made them forget the reason they were here. Caroline took the gun off James and held her hand out for some cartridges, opening the gun and loading both barrels, she then placed the open gun over the crook of her arm.

'Come on then,' she indicated with a nod towards Tom and Aled. 'You stay here, you won't be able to move quickly enough if anything happens,' she said to James, telling him to wait for the police. Tom and Aled opened the gate and went ahead of Caroline, across the first section of field.

'Where did you see it first?'

'Let's go and see if there is anything obvious around there.' Tom seemed a little hesitant to lead the way, the three of them on high alert for sight and sound of this creature that had been seen. Even Tom was somewhat doubting his own eyes.

They reached the tree that Tom had said it was spraying against, Caroline immediately bent down to smell the rough bark. She had no qualms about this, she said as she regularly smelt mares on her little stud farm, being able to tell if the mare was in season or not and ready for the stallion. She spent a minute or so smelling before announcing, 'Yep, cat pee smell, I suppose it would be wouldn't it?'

Tom and Aled were standing behind her, beady eyes looking around as if expecting to be pounced on any minute. 'Come on, let's go to where you think you saw it,' said Caroline again, indicating with the gun towards the woodland, prowling along cautiously as if she had kidnapped both men. They both went ahead, Tom leading the way, both men looking ahead and to each side whilst Caroline bought up the rear. 'Do these things climb trees?'

Both men stopped in their tracks. 'Shit,' said Aled, 'Never thought of that!' They continued walking like SAS officers through the undergrowth, but terrified lest they actually saw it.

'It could be less than ten feet away from us in all this bramble and bracken,' said Tom, adding almost as an afterthought, 'In fact Caroline, you swap places and go first.'

'Why, are you scared?' she asked.

'Well if truth be told, I'm more scared of you shooting me in the arse by mistake,' he answered.

'Fair comment,' she said, simultaneously looking up and seeing a helicopter circling ahead. 'Who's that?' she said.

'Looks like the local police helicopter,' said Aled, who would through his coastguard work no doubt be familiar with this type of aircraft.

'Hello,' shouted a voice, 'Hello,' it was coming from back by the gate, but it wasn't James. They turned around, having been defeated anyway by the thickening undergrowth and the thought that this creature whatever it was, may well be watching them from above in a tree. They strode across towards the gate, coming to meet a policeman in uniform. Caroline was a little conscious of the fact that she was actually carrying a twelve- bore shotgun, though the policeman totally ignored it. James had the license not Caroline.

'Hi, I've come to ask you to step back now and return to the gate, I'm the Police Wildlife Crime Officer for the area, I believe you think you have seen a big cat?' Caroline sensed Tom bristle as he said, 'I don't think I've seen a big cat; I know I've seen it; it was huge, dark brown- black, and bigger than a Labrador.'

'More than likely that what you have seen is a fully-grown male badger.'

'You're having a laugh aren't you", stated Tom looking open

mouthed in disbelief, I know the difference between a badger and a cat, and in all my years living here, I've never seen a badger, dead or alive. There are some up towards Holyhead, but never heard of any over here. Anyway, badgers don't spray up trees and have a tail that can reach way up behind them.'

The officer seemed to totally ignore his response, having clearly made up his mind. The cars at the gate had been joined now by another four-by-four, out of this came Iorwerth Davies and another two guys who both carried cased guns over their shoulders. How on earth had they heard of this? thought Aled, the grapevine here-abouts was amazing.

'Hang on,' said the Officer. He headed off towards Iorwerth and his mates and following whatever he had said to them, they got back in the car and drove off, displaying a thumbs up through the back-passenger window towards Caroline.

The officer came back, 'The helicopter has picked up something on their FLIR camera, so I would ask you now to leave whatever it is alone, as its far more likely as I said, to be a badger.' Caroline had already taken a dislike to the man, he appeared to be arrogant but, in her opinion, had no idea about wildlife.

'What's a FLIR camera?' asked Tom as he turned towards Aled, 'It's just what they call the heat seeking camera they have on board the helicopter.'

'So, what now?" asked Caroline as she went through the gate and stood next to James.

'The tall bloke with Iorwerth lives near Penmon, says he'll come back late at night, he has infra-red sights and a silencer on his rifle, though I'm not sure really how I actually feel about them shooting whatever it is.'

'No, I agree, but on the other hand I don't want any of my horses attacked, or any people for that matter. Mind you I hope they don't shoot one of our horses either,' said Caroline.

'Nor one of my ewes,' shouted Aled. Tom and Aled were standing together chatting, James joined them.

'Iorwerth told me that he knows there has been a big cat around for a while, but no one believes him. He saw it one night crossing the main road out of the village towards Beaumaris in the head-lights of his car, jumped the walls as if they weren't even there, then crossed the road in about two strides, but that was months ago apparently.'

'Do you reckon he did?' asked Aled, 'Maybe he had his beer goggles on, doesn't he like his pint?'

'He does,' said Tom, 'he always has a couple in the pub on an evening, but I've never seen him really bladdered and I've never seen him getting into his car, he always walks home. Other than that, he's usually in his tractor. Anyway, whatever I saw, is either well gone or it's laying low, I'll have a look online when I get home, to see if I can recognise anything similar to what I saw.'

Caroline and James got in the car, said their goodbyes and thank yous, reminding the two men to contact them if they saw anything like it again. They promised they would. Jo, Aled's wife had by then come down to join them, their little Jack Russel bitch tucked under her arm. They exchanged hello's and left the men to walk to their respective homes. Caroline drove down the lane to the beach front and turned around in the first convenient space, choosing to have a drive around the mares in the top fields while they were there. Doing it now would save a trip out later on.

All was well, most were sheltering from the flies under the canopy of a big old sycamore tree, which formed an umbrella above them, tucked close against a rock outcrop. They stood nose to tail, lazily flicking their tails at each other. They were totally relaxed and quietly confident, as Caroline walked amongst them scratching bottoms and the backs of ears, dependent on what end was presented to her first. This was mainly her little band of broodmares and this year's foals, only five, she rarely bred more than five a year. They would be weaned and bought home to the main yard towards the end of October, if the weather remained half decent, handled and then prepared for sale after Christmas, though there was actu-ally very little handling to do, so used were they to being touched and scratched, and having their legs and feet handled during their daily visits by Caroline and her business partner Emma.

Caroline walked back towards the gate. James had stayed in the vehicle, not really able to walk far these days, but was able to visit the stock when he ventured across the beach at low tide, in their scot-trac vehicle, a machine he had bought a few years previously, basically a cab and carrying area behind it which was built like a boat, it was tracked so could basically get everywhere, it was even designed to float like a boat with the tracks acting like paddles, though neither of them had been confident in its advanced age to test out this capability. James was able to pop along the beach, and around the other fields as and when he liked, and the horses were well used to his visit, normally with a few bales of hay in the back. When she got back to the yard, she finished the afternoon tasks and fed the horses that were stabled, mainly their stallions and bought the ones indoors, that had been turned out earlier in the day. The horse job never ended really, she would be out later that evening around nine o clock to top up haynet's and skip out, any dung produced in the intervening hours, it also gave an opportunity to check all was well with them, it was often the time of evening where a gut feeling or a little sign, would point out that a horse was maybe unwell or uncomfortable.

Chapter Seventeen

THE SOCO TEAM had been quite a time getting the man out of
the tree in the forestry, taking as many photos as were needed,
with the poor guy in situ. A large amount of blood had been
found once they started looking for it, it had spread downstream
in a tiny rivulet, and a considerable amount was around the base
of the tree and on the trunk. Clearly quite a scuffle had taken
place.

A few discernible sets of footprints had been found, but likely
the victim's own, the other, the young ladies. One set walking into
the area, the other, walking out. More than anything, there were
hoofed scuff marks cutting into the ground where the horse had
spun, then galloped off towards home, cutting deep with its shod
hooves into peaty ground, amidst the more solid outcrops of rock.
The fire brigade had been called to assist with the removal, but even
that was quite an effort with ingenuity, ropes and pulleys. As they'd
not been able to actually get a rescue unit anywhere near, the
method was less than pretty, thought Huws.

The fire team had been chosen carefully by their superior, a
more experienced crew, who had seen a few more nasty incidents
than the younger members. They had been useful, to help stretcher

the body back to the road where Jones the local undertaker was waiting with the black van.

'Second in less than a week, bad do,' he said, softly spoken as were most funeral directors he had met. 'Straight to Bangor again?'

'Yes please,' answered Huws. 'I'll follow you.' Huws left the scene and drove the short distance to the forest gate. Eric Mansell was there waiting to close it behind him. Huws wound down his window. 'There are others from the team still on scene and will need to get through later.'

'Yes, I will keep an eye out for them and open and close as needed, I'll keep it shut because if I don't, we will have every Tom Dick and Harry wandering about in here, I can't stop them walking in though. Cars, I can stop."

Huws had no doubt that this man could stop cars coming up the track, he wouldn't like to meet him on a dark night anywhere, but he seemed honest and straight enough.

'I will send someone over tomorrow to talk to Jenny,' Huws added. 'I doubt she has any more to say to you than she has already told you,' he answered gruffly, already half way back to his car.

Huws took the ten-minute drive to the community centre to think what his next step might be. Two murders in almost as many days and aged human remains, with very little evidence to connect the three, but nothing could be discounted. He would have a bit more detail on the bones in a couple of days, but Emyr Rowlands had warned him it may not be that useful, they could no doubt age the bones, but less likely know how long it had been there. He knew also that some of his team were following up on leads on the scraps of clothing that were with him, contacting the manufacturers, to see if they could possibly get a bit of a clue as to when the clothing would have been manufactured and sold. They may know a bit more in a couple of days. That may well give confirmation that it was the man they suspected him to be.

He pushed open the double doors into the entrance foyer, then the second lot of doors into the main space of the room. There was a scuffling of chairs, anticipation in the air as they waited for more news now on the second murder.

'Do we have a serial killer in the area?' said a voice from the back.

'Let's not speculate about anything at the moment, but you have obviously been told about this second victim. I'm off to the morg now, and as soon as I'm able I will be back with more details, but for the time being keep up with the work concerning Sarah Jones.' He turned towards the door, but added, 'Pritchard, you come with me.' Noticing his young detective sergeant's face actually blanching.

'Yes Sir,' he answered as he pushed papers into a pile on his desk and shut down his laptop. Huws was already in his car, when Pritchard emerged, he had managed to find a space outside, too early for the pub goers to have arrived as yet.

'Sorry Sir, just needed a pee before we go.'

Huws didn't have a lot to say on the way to Bangor, only twenty minutes or so away over the bridge crossing the Strait, dependent on the traffic, though most of the volume of traffic would be people coming home from work, from the mainland onto the island now, unlikely to be any significant ferry traffic just then.

He took the Hospital exit off the roundabout and made his way around the back. Pritchard had been particularly quiet all the way, like himself, not the biggest fan of autopsies. Huws tried to put him at ease by saying, 'Look lad, I need you there, if only to take down some notes while I watch, no way will I remember everything that Rowlands has to say.'

This produced a bit of a thankful release of breath from his young sidekick, possibly feeling he could concentrate on the note-writing, as opposed to what was unfolding on the table in front of him. He had been to just a couple of them before, the one bit he absolutely hated was when they opened the skull to expose the brain with the bone saw really turned his stomach. The rest of it he could cope with.

'Right,' said Emyr Rowlands, sounding less bright than he had a tendency to be. 'Let's get on with it shall we? Male, identified as a Mr Philip Morrison aged 51, address as per his ID in his wallet, driving license, bank card, RAC card, Cadnant gardens annual permit, as recorded on scene and in a bag over there.'

He directed a nod towards an evidence bag on the stainless-steel table against the wall.

'Found today, hanging suspended on the branches of a pine tree in Pentraeth forest, considerable amount of blood at scene due to exsanguination, following a catastrophic injury to the neck.'

This is stuff that Huws knew already, a furtive glance at Pritchard saw him head down busy writing in his pocket book, keeping his gaze very much away from what was going on the other side of the glass. Huws left him to it, aware of how the young DS would be feeling at this moment. Jane the assistant was busy, photographing the body as directed, every angle, every mark and bruise. This continued for the next thirty minutes, samples were taken, organs were weighed, and facts recorded as Rowlands continued with a running commentary throughout.

Eventually, he nodded in their direction, behind the glass, as he turned and directed Jane to undo his apron strings. He removed his gloves and left the room. Huws and Pritchard made their way towards the office and waited for Rowlands to reappear.

'What do we have then?' asked Huws as Rowlands sat down opposite him.

'Ok let's start by giving you a bit of information with regards to your skeleton. I'm afraid we don't have a lot of information from the tests, other than he was a male, as we already knew, in his forties possibly and the nearest guestimate we can come up with is that he could well have lain there for two years or more. Does this match with anything you have come up with your end? We're also awaiting results from a dental database search.'

Huws nodded, Pritchard continued to write his notes, slightly pinker around the gills now than he had been fifteen minutes previously. This information could well tie up with their missing persons' records search.

'Right,' continued Rowlands, 'What we have presented to us today, I would say definitely ties in with our previous case only a matter of days ago. A brutal frenzied murder. A death caused by severe blood-loss, no doubt leading to a cardiac arrest. From evidence at scene, the body was likely dragged up into the tree post mortem, by I would imagine a system of ropes and pulleys, similar in fact to how he was taken down. I obviously have no idea why someone would want to do such a thing. Some sort of ritual act maybe.

He has severe lacerations to the neck, most of his neck structures having been ripped away, leaving his neck vertebrae exposed at the base of his skull, down as far as C6 which is virtually the whole of the length of his neck. X ray results will confirm the fact that I found significant damage to the bone and multiple bone fractures. If he hadn't bled to death, he would no doubt have died due to damage at an upper level to his neural breathing control centre. Extensive bruising on the arms and upper torso shows a fair struggle took place, defence wounds more than likely, clothes torn. In my mind this is either a machete, or axe, but we need to put more work into our findings as yet.

The torso in this case was intact, all organs still in place and undamaged, so mainly head, neck and upper back area. Attacked from behind I would imagine. I doubt with that degree of initial damage that he would have been able to put up much of a fight, poor sod. Whoever is doing this is quite possibly the most vicious killer I have come across, and that's saying something, having seen some fairly brutal murders in my time. I was involved on the periphery during the Peter Moore murders in the mid-nineties, he was a real twisted bastard. We need to get this person behind bars as soon as we can, before you have another death on your hands. Whoever it is clearly knows the area really well, and knows his way around, knowing the places locally that not many people go to, but also, particularly in Sarah's case not going out of their way to cover their tracks, as in hide the bodies. It's almost as if they are out to get maximum shock effects.'

He nodded his thanks. Pritchard was still nose in his pocket notebook.

'You can stop writing now lad,' said Huws. 'Got all we need for now. Let's get back to base and give them the news, we need to step up now before this madman strikes again.'

'Why madman and not a madwoman?' asked Pritchard.

'Good point', said Huws as he pulled at the vape, people always said madman as opposed to mad women, although through history there had been women murderers as well, like Myra Hyndley, Beverley Allitt and of course Rose West, but it did seem to him though, that women generally worked hand in hand with their husbands or boyfriends, supposedly in the name of love. It made for an interesting discussion with his junior as they returned to the village hall.

Chapter Eighteen

IT WAS a beautiful early autumn day, a little nip in the air, but still some heat in the sun, the views from the yard were glorious. When Caroline and James first saw the smallholding one September day in ninety- three, they fell in love with it immediately, totally blanking all the negatives that were likely to belong to it. They were smitten. The house was small, but rooms could be knocked into one, cowsheds attached which could obviously be made into useable stables, an old rusting Dutch barn could be replenished with a coat of paint, as could the cowshed below it.

The fields fell away from the buildings towards the beach below, becoming progressively boggier the nearer the sea they got. There must have been a good fifty acres of swampland covered in bull-rushes between their land and the sea, a conservation project maybe they thought, but over the years the reality was that it was impos-sible to rectify. Dreams of draining their land out into the swamp would never materialise, on finding that if they opened ditches it simply allowed the swamp to disgorge its sour brackish water onto their fields. Behind the cottage was the vast Pentraeth forestry, planted way back in the fifties covering Mynydd Llwydiarth. This forestry gave shelter from all but the most direct Northerly winds, a micro climate being formed protecting them. The disadvantage however, it blocked off any sunshine between November and March, meaning they lived in shadow through the winter months, something they had learnt to live with. They had between them built the stud farm up over the years, renting extra land as it grew and was needed.

Today Caroline needed to take a couple of mares along the beach to the other parcel of land. It was foal weaning time and the mares would be well out of earshot of the anxious whinnying foals. They were well handled, so she knew from previous experience that they would soon settle down. Her mother Mary often helped her with tasks on the yard and would be more than capable of leading one of the mares along the beach.

Headcollars on, both mares were taken out of their stables with James on hand to shut the top doors, for fear of foals making a bid for freedom over the stable doors. Caroline and Mary set off down the drive, both mares neighing in response to the calls of their offspring. The route along the beach was a full mile and a half, but a lot shorter than taking the steep hill up to the village of Allt Goch, and down again to the beach along the road, risking traffic.

As the mares entered the beach, the novelty of the sand under their feet caused them to promptly lose interest in the fading calls of their foals. They skittered playfully through puddles of receding sea water, the tide already well out. They took a shortcut over the salt-ings necessitating a few nimble jumps over the odd welly sucking hole. The mares curling around the women, playfully jogging along, no doubt also remembering and anticipating the freedom of fresh fields. On this last matter they would be disappointed as Caroline always put them on relatively bare ground for a couple of weeks post weaning to help dry up their milk flow, followed then by a move to fresh pasture to enjoy the last of the autumn grass before the winter months set in.

Today they were going to be put in the very fields that neighbour Tom had supposedly seen his black creature a few days before. Nothing seemed to have come of that, but she did suspect that Iorwerth and his mates may well have been around during the interim nights with their rifles and night sights. They were sensible country people though, and she was perfectly confident that they would not be doing the same once they knew that she had got some horses on the fields. She would however ring Iorwerth later just to give him the heads up.

The track off the beach was in sight, a sandy passageway with almost a tunnel of bramble growth allowing them through. The brambles would soon die off as the winter settled in, in fact, she would clear some of them, with her regular trips along the beach during the winter months with big bales of hay for the outwintering horses, pushing her way through with the front loader and bale spike on her tractor. They emerged onto the lane, just a couple of hundred metres of lane now before they came to the field gates.

From their left as if timed to the second, appeared James in the old Range Rover, ready to pick them up and drive them home to save the walk back. Caroline walked in front, her mare the strongest and boldest of the two, still jogging in anticipation of freedom, short memories clearly, foals totally forgotten.

Suddenly, the mare snorted and in straightening up allowed Caroline a clear view of the lane ahead. No more than two hundred metres ahead lay a huge big cat, its length including tail taking up the width of the country lane, it was focused on something on the other side of the sparse hedge. Both women froze, Mary had clearly seen it too, the mares like statues. James behind, a slightly higher viewpoint, simply gazed out the windscreen, as Caroline looked back to see if he had noticed. Obviously, he had, he was open mouthed.

Stupidly, they both started walking towards it, dragging reluctant ponies behind them, Caroline was actually doubting what she was seeing, was it actually just a large dog? Maybe a figment of her imagination, something she was watching on television from the comfort of her sofa. Mary followed. Within seconds the cat got up and loped up the road, took a right at a bank and off it went into a young plantation.

Caroline turned and looked at her mother, James bringing up the rear, speechless. This was clearly what Tom had seen, and although she had no real reason to doubt he was telling the truth, until you have seen things with your own eyes, you still can't believe what you have been told. She called back to James, 'What do we do with these ponies, do we take them back home?'

'Only you can decide that,' he shouted back through the window. 'Most of the other horses are on the hill, I can't see much benefit in just taking these two home, I'm sure whatever it was will be well gone by now, don't you think?'

'Well gone?' shouted Caroline. 'Do you reckon! It was a huge big cat, not a pussy cat, where the hell has it come from? Did you not see it properly?' She was getting scared now, the reality of what they had just seen sinking in.

'Of course, I saw it, but like you I have no idea where It's come from, so come on, get those mares up to the top fields instead of here at the bottom, and we will get home, I will ring a couple of people for advise when I get back.'

Chapter Nineteen

IDRIS HUWS STOOD outside the village hall, looking more like a fifty's youth than a Detective Inspector. Leaning on the wall, one knee bent, foot up on the plasterwork, vape in hand producing clouds of white with every puff. The collar of his by now unfashionable mackintosh, up against the increasing autumnal breeze.

The village was placed quite high for an Anglesey location, catching the winds from whichever direction it blew, it got hard hit by winter snows as well from what he'd been told, blowing straight across from the Carneddau Hills directly opposite, on the mainland. He hoped to god he wasn't still going to be here come winter.

Lunchtime and evening business seemed to have picked up in the pub next door, since they had taken over the room at the start of the murder case. No doubt more a case of the villagers having a nosey at what may be going on. He had spoken to the landlord a couple of times in the last couple of weeks, being a local councillor and on the Coastguard team, Michael seemed to know most people in his area, but even he had drawn a blank as to any ideas. He thought that he may pop in later that evening, to see who was about, and have a chat with a few people, not something he was in the

habit of doing but he had nothing else to go on, other positive identification regarding the remains in the quarry. The only questions
regarding that, had been some deep scores on the femur bones, but
the pathologist had put that down to time and tide, and gnawing by
animals, somehow it still didn't sit that well with him. They had
managed to get hair, and finger and toe nail samples from the body,
these however had given no indication as to the person having used
drugs prior to death.

Due to the fact that most of the flesh had gone, any other clues
regarding how he may have committed suicide had drawn a blank.
However, the parents would be able to give their son a burial and
get closure.

He pocketed the vape and headed indoors. Once through the
double doors, the coldness of the room hit him, inefficient radiators
heating up a poorly insulated high ceiling, most of the team wearing
their coats. They sat at their makeshift desks, folding tables that
would no doubt have been used for village celebrations, on metal
tubular stacking seats with plastic banding across them, they would
be considered 'Retro' or 'vintage' by his wife, maybe even quite
valuable. She would love to get her hands on some of these to sell
on her Etsy page. She seemed to spend her time sourcing stuff like
this now, since she started her new hobby. She had mentioned more
than once, her desire once he had done his thirty years-service, that
they sell their suburban semi and buy somewhere with outbuildings,
for her renovating and furniture selling. Mm, was all he could think
to that.

He looked at the team, heads down tip tapping away at their
laptops, wires running across the room to the various extension
leads that were set up for the duration. He had to admit that he was
useless with modern technology and watching some of the team
bringing page after page of information, mostly police classified
stuff up on their screens within seconds of a request, just totally
baffled him, it made his brain hurt. He however, never let them
realise this.

No one had come up with anything yet, not a single lead

regarding the two cases, Sarah Jones and Philip Morrison still lay in a fridge in the local Morgue. Other than the similarity in their injuries, they had made no headway in finding their killer, or indeed killers.

He had been well taught by his seniors over the years to never presume the obvious. His team were still attempting to follow every single idea put in front of them, regarding people's movements around the time of both murders. Every local inhabitant had been spoken to, second home owners had been checked out, cottage agents, had in some cases, reluctantly given out contact details of visitors, and self-catering cottage owners had given out contact details of their cleaners, to follow up on any possibilities that they may have found something unexpected.

Only one cottage owner had announced that they had a strange couple staying with them at the time, who had left a disgusting mess, causing them to have had to postpone their next customers, to give them extra time to clean up. Traces of blood had been found resulting in a phone call to the police. A visit by SOCO found more blood on an exposed bit of stonework in the sitting room. They were discounted following investigation led to the arrest of the male of the partnership for domestic abuse, which he admitted, occurred during his stay at the beachside cottage.

Huws supposed that if someone chooses to rent out their property to total strangers, then you really have no idea whatsoever who they might be. He sat at his desk in the back room, he was in and out so often that no one seemed to bother to heat it. He looked for any memos that may have been placed on his desk but as had been the case the last few days; nothing. The clock on the wall said 7:30 p.m., but it had said that every day since he had moved his team in here. He looked at his watch, nearly 6 p.m. He would send most of the team home in a bit, totally pointless them freezing their bits off overnight, particularly as they were all contactable and didn't live a million miles away. One bobby on his nightshift could come and check-up the building later on.

In the meantime, he would scroll through the work to date on the laptop on his desk, maybe in the hope that something would jump out from the words in front of him.

Chapter Twenty

IDRIS WALKED INTO THE PUB, the door led straight into the main bar area, with a larger room off to each side. The air was fuggy, no doubt due to the large open fire at one end needing a sweep, causing warm smoke to hang in the rafters. As soon as he walked in the room fell silent. The few people at the bar suddenly finding something of great interest in the bottom of their pint glasses. He smiled to himself, it would always happen, and it reminded him of the old film Wicker man, when a police officer was sent to a lonely Scottish island, to investigate the disappearance of a child, and all the locals clammed up. He thought it may have been released in the early seventies, when he himself was probably too young to have watched it.

'Good Evening DI Huws, what shall I get you?' asked Michael the landlord, breaking the silence.

'A pint of your best please,' he answered and stepped across to an empty stool at the bar. Michael took a glass from the overhead shelf, checked it against the light and gave it an extra polish with his tea-towel. He recognised the chap sitting at the end of the bar sideways on, using the wall behind him to lean on. This was the man whom he had spoken to outside the village hall, earlier on in the investigation, Iorwerth, if he remembered rightly. Check shirt and flat cap, comfortable and at home in his surroundings.

'Good evening Iorwerth,' he offered in his friendliest tone of voice. He didn't get what the answer was, it was so mumbled, in fact poor Iorwerth didn't look at all comfortable that he had been seemingly singled out for a conversation. He stared into his beer glass. The others at the bar had slowly melted away, found chairs to sit on around the rest of the room, collected in little clusters. Far enough away not to be drawn into an unwanted conversation, but close enough to eavesdrop. Huws reckoned there were as many women as men, which was reasonably unusual at tea time in a village pub, but he did know by now ,that there were a few clubs that used the pub. Members of community choirs and knitting groups, that had been usurped from the village hall, when they took it over and infringed their rights to be there. Seemingly the village Chapel had been commandeered for this purpose, and likely just as cold as the Hall.

'Any developments on the awful incidents Sir?' asked Michael, as he passed him his beer. Huws, paused, he was not at all keen to divulge to the non-looking but listening customers at the bar, that all they had come up with so far, was a big fat zilch.

'We have a couple of leads we are working on at the moment.' Michael nodded and winked at him, his nod however was aimed towards Iorwerth in the corner, though Iorwerth had his head down staring into his pint glass, which had just been refilled for him by another customer. Huws imagined it was likely, that a regular such as Iorwerth rarely paid for his pint, being well liked in the village meant a pint was automatically pulled for him when someone came through the door. Huws hoped he might initiate a chat with the old boy, but he wasn't holding his breath. '

Getting chillier now,' said Huws, with a nod towards Iorwerth. Iorwerth looked up at him and you could almost hear his brain whirring as he nodded, his rheumy blue eyes seeming to bore right into Huws's soul.

'Yes.' A pause. 'The smell of autumn soil is in the air now,' he replied sagely, returning his gaze to the bottom of his pint glass. Huws noticed it was actually a glass tankard engraved with the old boy's name. He must be well thought of hereabouts.

'Petrichor,' mumbled Iorwerth.

'Beg your pardon?' reacted Huws.

'Petrichor, a word for the earthy aroma of rain falling onto dry summer earth.' Huws just nodded, so surprised was he that the man had used such a word.

'Mm yes,' more to show Iorwerth that he wasn't unfamiliar with the word. 'Did you hear about Eifion's yearling bullock?' asked Iorwerth, leaning forward on his stool so he could lower his voice slightly. Huws straightened and stepped forward to hear.

'A bullock?' answered Huws.

'Yes, a young castrated male bull steer,' he added. 'I know what a bullock is man, I meant, what about it?'.

'Eifion along the beach, thought the other day it had been stolen. It was missing from the herd, John that works for him had a wander all around the boundary, it was actually over a low wall on the seaward side of his land.'

'I'd heard about this, I reckon he had been butchered and the meat sold, you hear of that being done in the North West of England don't you, particularly with sheep, only the fleeces left in a pile complete with skins. Gets sold on the black market then.' interrupted Michael who had clearly sidled towards Iorwerth in order to eavesdrop.

'No, absolutely no way,' cut in Iorwerth. 'I picked it up over the wall with my JCB, and put it on the knacker wagon, it had not been butchered properly, the flesh had been ripped off it, they clearly had a very blunt Cleaver, or it wasn't done by a person.' He turned back to his pint, lifting it in Huws's direction, indicating a refill. Huws obliged. Iorwerth was deep in thought, shaking his head.

'Worth quite a bit too, a loss, a young steer like that.' He nodded.

'Did this Eifion report it to the police?' asked Huws.

'Duw no, pointless really, it would probably take them a week to turn up to a call about a bullock,' said Iorwerth, staring him straight in the eye, almost accusing him of police negligence, as if he himself was solely responsible for the entire North Wales Police force.

'Where will the carcase be now? Surely the insurers will want to send someone out to see it'.

'Gaerwen incinerator, more than likely it will be ash, by now.' Iorwerth slurped the last of his pint, wiped his mouth with the back of his hand and got up to leave. Huws looked around, noticing that the group sat directly behind him had clearly been awaiting a reaction, failing to observe, one they had gone back to their chatter and pints.

As Iorwerth left with a touch to his cap, which Huws suspected may well be welded to his scalp, a group appeared at the door, chattering away, only to shut up immediately they noticed him at the bar. There you go, wicker man mentality again, he thought to himself with a wry smile. Around twelve people in all came in, most of them immediately bagging a table in either of the side rooms, clearly preparing to eat. Some hung around the bar and ordered drinks with Michael, well, actually they didn't order drinks that he heard anyway. It seemed that Michael knew them all and knew what their drink of choice was. Michael must have noticed his interest.

'Local Community Choir members,' he offered. 'These are the regulars who take advantage of our Curry for a fiver night, you've kicked them out of the village hall where they usually gather, they have to go into the Chapel now, mind you by all accounts it is warmer in there.'

Huws's ears pricked up at the words Curry night, his wife Gwen had something on tonight, it was her Merched y Wawr group and would no doubt be late home, by the time they had washed up the cups and saucers and put the world to rights.

'Can I order a curry please, not anything too hot,' he asked Michael, who nodded and shouted,

'Another Korma,' through into the kitchen.

'Half and half?' With a nod, Huws decided to take himself

through into the left- hand room, the fire had settled now, there must be more draw through the chimney, and the smoky fug had lessened slightly. Its why he and Gwen had chosen a log burner for themselves, less smoke and ash mess. He found a small table in the front corner, took his coat off and settled down with his pint. He had refused a second beer, choosing instead a pint of J2O to keep him occupied.

A young waitress bought through his Curry, a shop bought jar of Mango chutney besides the plate, cutlery rolled up in a paper napkin. No unnecessary finesse, which added pounds to the cost of a meal in any restaurant just a couple of miles away in Beaumaris, but he was pleased to find that the curry was well cooked, and tasty.

He enjoyed people watching, when he was out and about, but it was never the same when people knew you were in the force, it would have been around the pub in an instance, people always minded what they said. He felt sadness sometimes these days, when he had joined the job, policemen were respected, people to look to for help and advice. Nowadays sadly they were looked upon as some sort of enemy, not in all quarters he understood, but by many. These good people of the village that were here this evening, he knew, would be disappointed at their seeming lack of progress, particularly on the young Sarah Jones case as she was local. Poor Morrison was a newcomer, and hadn't really integrated himself into village life, wasn't as well known, not that anyone was less sympathetic. He could certainly at this moment, guarantee that he and his team were being judged by the gathering in this hostelry.

People were talking in whispers, the occasional raucous laugh erupting from the other room, only he knew, it was because he wasn't in there. This lot were behaving like a group of school-children afraid of a telling off from a stern teacher. He realised he would be unlikely to gain any snippets of information in here. He pushed his plate away, stood, grabbed his coat and prepared to leave. The bar room was fuller now, but the crowd parted like a pair of curtains to let him through. He was aware that as soon as he closed the door, relief would flood through amongst the punters. A fact driven home as he passed the windows of the room he had left and heard the same loud laughter as the other room, relief at his departure, a return to normality. He walked around the back of the pub to his car, the usual little group of smokers huddling underneath a wooden pergola festooned with finished hanging baskets, watching his departure.

'Definitely wicker man,' he smiled to himself.

Chapter Twenty-One

'HI CAROLINE,' said Aled, anxiety clear in his voice, which surprised her as he was usually so laid back, about everything.

'Jo has just come in and said that your horses seem to be a little disturbed in your top field, thought I ought to phone and let you know. I'll walk up the hill now and have a look, if you are going to make your way over.'

'Thanks,' said Caroline, already motioning James to get the car keys. 'We'll come along the beach; the tide is out. Thank you for letting us know.'

She stuck the phone in her back pocket, and grabbed a coat hanging in the utility as she went out. James was on her tail.

'What's up?' He made for the passenger seat, he was no fool, he knew Caroline would be in the driver's seat and off in a second if there was anything horsey kicking off.

'Probably nothing, but I'm a bit uncomfortable having seen the cat the other day. Jo reckons the horses are upset about something, Aled is off to have a look up the fields now. You said the lads had been keeping an eye out at night but hadn't seen anything, though didn't you?'

'Yeah, they've been there the last couple of nights, night vision binoculars and all the kit. They haven't seen hide nor hair of anything at all, not a fox, or even a local tom cat. They said it is strangely quiet, other than the horses mooching around.'

'You do trust them not to accidentally shoot any of the horses, don't you?'

'Of course, they won't, they know what they are doing, they have grown up hunting and shooting and their fathers before them, they also know the area like the back of their hands. Apparently, they have been there from dusk till dawn for a couple of nights now and zilch.'

'Ok, if you trust them then so do I, you said they had silencers too on their guns, so it wouldn't frighten the horses if they did shoot something.'

James nodded. Caroline got to the bottom of the drive, and checking ahead briefly, she drove onto the beach via the cut in the dune, through the soft entrance mud onto the firmer sand, as she went straight out through a gap in the saltings, before bearing a right towards the east end of Red Wharf bay. They knew the beach well now, but still knew to keep moving, the sand having the potential to be very soft in patches, many a vehicle had become trapped despite all efforts, and covered by the incoming tide which was amazingly fast as the beach was so huge and flat.

They crossed a number of small rivulets and were now driving along the edge of the saltings, which bordered the part of the beach that was usually busiest in the summer, due to the awarding of a blue flag for cleanliness. Further along the beach became more pebbly, giving way to a foreshore of stone. This is where she knew to keep to a certain angle and drive off the beach to the tarmac road.

They took a right and drove past Jean's beach café and the main car park before continuing on and up the hill. They passed by the entrance to Aled and Jo's Bryn Gwyn Bach, and around the next corner past the usually empty second home opposite the entrance to their top fields. She pulled the car into the gateway off the road and got out, already scanning the tops of the fields and seeing the horses in a tight group.

Before James had even got out of the car, Caroline was out and over the gate. Aled and Jo were already walking around the seaward boundary. Caroline had done a headcount and come up with nine, instead of ten, there was a foal missing and clearly the little bunch of mares were upset. They were all watching Aled and Jo, but Caroline sensed the heads up, alert ears and occasional snort was caused by more than the strangers in their field. Caroline started up the slope towards the bunch of mares and Aled and Jo turned back to follow her direction. She counted again and a third time, definitely one foal missing. Boo the grey mare's foal, Boo was in a muck sweat, yellow sweat stains marking her silver neck. Hang on, she thought as she moved amongst them, sensing the mares were keeping their foals close. She knew that even though these were mares she had owned for a long time, they could take fright in a second, one wrong move or sound. They were highly charged and on the alert. She could easily be trampled if they chose to take off.

Boo was injured, resting a hind leg, Caroline couldn't see an injury on her lower limb, but as her gaze travelled upwards, a huge open gouge down her flank from the croup down to the thigh was obvious, not one deep cut but three, that she could see from this side. This would need urgent attention. She moved around the back of the distressed mare, who was trembling, a mixture of injured shock and fear she guessed. There was a similar injury on her other quarter, this time causing significant damage to her vulva and anus.

A terrible thought crossed Caroline's mind as she shouted for James to phone the vet and bring a headcollar and rope from the car. In the late eighties and early nineties, there had been a sick twisted and up to now uncaught person who was maiming and killing horses, by doing unspeakable things to them, in the South East of England and East Anglia. Was this a similar thing? She certainly hoped not. Aled, Jo and James got to her at the same time, James blowing slightly from the exertion.

'The vet is on his way,' he gasped, handing her a headcollar. 'Shit, almighty,' he exclaimed catching sight of the injuries. 'How the hell did she do that? Has she been caught up somewhere?'

'No idea,' said Caroline, never one to cry but very close, 'Her foal is missing too, it must have got through the fence somewhere and she tried and maybe failed to follow? Can you hear a foal shouting anywhere Jo?'

'No, we haven't heard or seen anything, we walked the boundary and haven't seen any sign of it. Was it the pretty little bay speckly one?' asked Jo.

'I'll go and have another look,' said Aled, clearly not one for hanging around when he could be doing something more useful. 'I will have a look on our side of the boundary too, you are welcome to bring the mare up to the farm yard for the vet to deal with if you like.'

'Thanks Aled, but James will pop home in a minute and fetch the trailer, so once the vet has had an initial look here and maybe given her something for the pain, we will take her home, she'll be happier there than somewhere unfamiliar where she'll still hear her mates calling.'

Caroline was by now leading the bereft mare towards the top gate, the vet knew to bring his van to the pull in that James, minutes ago vacated. She would be happy standing by the gate with her friends nearby. They were starting to relax a little by now in the presence of familiar people, though the two older mares were still very alert to their surroundings and were keeping guard.

Dafydd Williams the vet pulled up in his van, mobile phone to his ear, no doubt the surgery telling him of some other emergency that needed his attention. He pulled on his faded green overalls and opened the gate, with a nod of acknowledgement, never one for needless small talk and gossip. Caroline held the mare as Dafydd slipped his hand over her back, as he approached her quarters for fear of scaring her. He looked, then moved the mares bloodied tail aside as he passed to her other side. The mare was getting cold now, and out of instinct and love for her animals Caroline took off her jacket and placed it over the mare's loins for some warmth.

'Did you see anywhere the mare could have been caught up?' asked Dafydd.

'No, well I haven't looked but my neighbours did, and the foal is still missing, we haven't found it anywhere, unless its managed to get through somewhere and onto the hill. It's strange though that it isn't shouting because its separated.'

Dafydd just nodded, 'Mm, these injuries are strange. I don't think they're wire injuries, Equal scores down both sides and clearly it caught her vulva too, that is a nasty injury and we'll certainly need to debride it and freshen it a little so that I can stitch it up.'

'James will be here in just a bit with the trailer to take her home, she is one of our only ones that hates travelling, loading her here might not be straightforward,' said Caroline.

'I can give her some intravenous bute for the pain and just a small amount of sedative now then to settle her.'

Dafydd was always efficient and rarely had Caroline ever seen him panic, she knew that he would never take unnecessary risks, he always proceeded with caution and would, she knew, always ask someone superior if he had doubts. He had never let her down.

Then Aled shouted from the other side of the hedge. 'It's here, I have found the foal, well sort of,' he added. Caroline looked at Jo and asked her would she hold the mare for a minute. The mare standing quietly now, drowsy and slightly head down. Jo, she knew was wary of anything bigger than a sheep, but she cautiously took hold of the lead-rope as Caroline set off at a sprint.

'I'll shout if I need you down there Dafydd. James will be back any second to take over from Jo.'

Dafydd acknowledged her with a nod, still busy examining the wounds, no doubt working out the best way to stitch it together. As Caroline reached the hedge, where she could just see Aled through it, she asked him if it was ok or hurt. He replied that she may well not want to see the foal.

'I'm not squeamish, I've seen some pretty awful injuries over the years, with horses and other animals.'

'Oh, I don't doubt, I'm sure you are not, but this isn't really something that you are likely to have seen before. See the bottom of the hedge where you are now, I reckon it got through there.' She looked at a hole which looked to be a pathway for one of the many foxes that lived on the hillside.

'No way would a foal get through there?' she replied.

'No, I agree, unless it was already dead, and has been dragged through.' Silence, the possibility dawning on her.

'The cat, that bloody big cat that we saw.' The thought of this was like a direct punch in her stomach. 'You know something? Even though I've seen this it, it's like it happened in my imagination. Fucking hell, do you think the cat has killed it and attacked the mare for trying to protect her foal? The bastard, the utter bloody bastard. What do we do now?'

Aled had persuaded her not to come around to his side of the hedge, but said he would dispose of the remains, as they were. In fact, he told Caroline that all that remained of the foal was one hind quarter section. There was nothing else to be found, he did not want to have her seeing it for herself. No doubt this would be the stuff of nightmares for her for a fair while. Caroline returned to the top gate, James by now manoeuvring the trailer in the lane so it was up against one bank, lessening the chances of the mare evading the box, though he had noted that she was fairly dopey, needing great care on the journey home.

'Christ, you look as if you have seen a ghost,' said James as he looked across at Caroline. He knew his wife was a tough cookie, but she had clearly been crying.

'We need to bring all these mares and foals' home so they are safer, that cat has killed and eaten most of the foal.'.

Dafydd raised his head. 'Cat?'

'Yes,' said James, 'A few of us saw what could only have been a big cat, not very long ago. I'm surprised you haven't heard already, in your line of work. We called the police and they sent a helicopter out with a heat seeking device on it, and although it picked up something in the undergrowth behind the beach café, the Police wildlife liaison bloke was determined that what Tom next door saw was a badger. Since then though we've seen it, Caroline, myself and the mother in law. We saw it as clear as you are standing here now.'

'One of the old boys that Aled sees in the pub swears he has seen it too, said he caught sight of it crossing the main road towards Beaumaris in the headlights of his car. He and his shooting buddies have been out looking for it at night,' added Jo. Dafydd shook his head in disbelief.

'I don't know what to say. I've heard all sorts of stories here-abouts, but always assumed people were mistaken, but I will say that these injuries on Boo, are indeed compatible with what I would imagine a big cat would inflict by jumping on the mare's quarters. Caroline, James, you take the mare home, go slow with her around those bends at the top. I'll have a look over there with Aled and follow you on. Put her in an empty stable for now and just get some buckets of warm water ready for me, I can get to work on her straight away, the sooner the better.'

Chapter Twenty-Two

DAFYDD WORKED his magic over the next hour, intricate work, the mare deeply sedated but not enough that she couldn't remain on her feet, head down swaying slightly, though supported lightly on each side, by Caroline and Emma her business partner who had driven over it seemed at the speed of light once she had been phoned with the dreadful news.

Dafydd freshened up the already drying edges of the wounds, gently with a scalpel after an injection of local anaesthetic, in order to have live tissue to pull together. These sorts of wounds were always difficult to heal. Post injury soft tissue swelling made stitches break down. Granulation tissue would very likely form. That would need to be dealt with again further down the line. Drain tubes inserted to allow for the residual pus, following almost inevitable infection, to drain away. Her vulva and rectum had almost become one gaping orifice, never the cleanest site to work with. They would need to fight this injury from inside and out. It was likely to end her ability to breed again.

Whilst this was ongoing, Caroline had asked James to phone four of her horse savvy friends, to come and help her fetch the remaining mares and foals from their fields and walk them along the beach to be closer to the yard. Thankfully this was a walk the mares were well used to and were sensible enough to behave. They had just enough time before the tide would totally cover the beach.

After Dafydd had finished, he left her with a pile of antibiotic medication, and pain killing sachets of Bute. Boo, was settled on a deep clean bed and rugged up. The mare was by now very subdued after her obvious ordeal. Had she been a human, Caroline would have said that she was in that initial stage of deep grief after a huge loss. By the early evening, as the days were now getting shorter, all the broodmares and foals were at home in the front fields.

Normally the bringing of the mares and foals' home, along the beach usually in later October for weaning, was a case of great jollity. Mares jig jogging along sideways, foals who had spent a summer growing up as a little bunch of terrors, taking chances and doing individual high tailed scoots along the beach, sometimes going way ahead of their mother, then suddenly noticing their solitary position in the middle of the vast beach, only to hurtle back legs akimbo, lowering themselves to the ground in an uncoordinated gallop effort, to make an embarrassed return to the fold. This would happen many times on the stretch of sand between the top fields and the home farm, giving Caroline a chance to see which foals showed some promise regarding agility and bravery.

Today it seemed a far more sombre affair, foals sticking close to their dams quarters, walking along the beach in a line, akin to a giant centipede, with interspersed large and small segments, the last foal bringing up the rear. They came off the beach through the cut in the dune and up the drive. Before Caroline had them led into the field underneath the cottage, she had a quick once over the mares and foals, for any other missed injuries but thankfully, none were found, the mares were released into the field. Caroline was glad that all her stock was now close by and easy to see.

Two days later, all hell let loose, the local paper had caught the story, there it was in black and white, a front-page headline with a half page on page three.

'PAWS. Just as you thought it was safe to go on holiday'.

A headline with a photo of a snarling panther, page three headline was, 'Is there a Panther on the prowl.'

The full story was there, a police spokesman describing their search, and the involvement of the helicopter, the description of the injured mare. Caroline smiled to herself, another local horse owner had announced that her horse also had similar injuries, though when Caroline had previously warned her about the existence of a big cat, she had laughed. Their phone was on fire all day, though thankfully James dealt with it. Being a newspaper editor in a previous life before they met, this was right up his street.

Caroline had checked Boo thoroughly that morning, she seemed fine in herself, but had refused point blank to eat the medicated feed she had been given for her breakfast. Caroline had therefore mixed the painkilling powder with warm water and given her that orally with a syringe. The antibiotic was more of an issue, but a phone call to the vet's surgery had prompted Dafydd to change the powders for an intramuscular daily injection, which Caroline was happy to do. She would fetch the necessities later when she had finished mucking out.

A quick scan down across the field saw the mares and foals grazing in a huddle, one mare as is often the case, on lookout for predators, something that horses had never stopped doing despite domestication. Maybe they had been right all along, there were lions out there. It certainly seemed so. Caroline's mother Mary, had taken an interest in helping with the horses, when she and her husband William, Caroline's father, had moved to live at the farm, finished the yard, with a last tidy of the muck heap.

Emma, was off today, but was aware of what went on the previous day, having been one of the first people that James had contacted to come to help.

'Coffee,' called James through the front window. On entering the cottage, the phone rang. James answered, he appeared to be having an animated conversation about the cat. Mary and Caroline sat down with their drinks. James held the phone away from his ear, putting his palm over the mouthpiece.

'The BBC wildlife person is on the phone, not David Attenborough obviously, he added with a half-smile, but the local guys from the BBC office in Bangor. He wants to come over this afternoon and have a chat with us. Is that ok with you?'

'Well yes, I suppose it is,' answered Caroline, realising probably for the first time, the enormity of what had actually happened.

Chapter Twenty-Three

'IFAN PUW,' he said as he got out of the battered looking old Skoda estate. 'BBC Wildlife programme coordinator for Wales.' He offered a hand, which James shook. He looked a kind, simple soul, bearded and a tad Bill Oddy-ish, thought Caroline. Crinkled, well-worn and stained Barbour jacket and corduroy trousers, tucked in to his colourful socks, disappearing into a pair of ancient looking leather walking boots.

Out of the other side of the car, the polar opposite of Ifan emerged, a tall, lanky smartly dressed man in his sixties, who was introduced as John Thompson.

'John here is a bit of an expert on wildlife tracking, he specialises in setting up infra-red cameras. We have caught film footage of many a British native creature with his help. We're hoping that you might allow us to place cameras in strategic positions, to see if we can catch sight of this big cat.' '

Do you believe us then?' asked James. 'The police seemed to think it was a bit of a dramatic hoax, though the vet took some photos of the mare's injuries before stitching them and sent them to the big cat expert at Chester Zoo. They came back with the verdict that the injuries were compatible with what they would expect of a big cat. The Police Wildlife Liaison Officer tried to convince us it was a badger. Must be a bloody big badger is all I can say. Caroline will show you the mare in a minute. We also have the remains of the foal, in a bag in the barn awaiting incineration.'

'Of course, I believe you,' he responded. 'I've seen them myself; I hate to think how many big cats of different species are wandering the wilds of the United Kingdom. I've seen them myself, on the foothills of Cader Idris, near where I live, in fact there are two there that I've seen together, though I have no idea whether they are male and female or the same sex. Time will tell on that score.'

Caroline, was pleased to hear this. She felt that no one would believe their bizarre sightings, certainly the police had made them feel like utter idiots.

'I'm so pleased you've seen it or indeed them too. Some people around here think I'm mad, but you know, the people who have, are sensible people, who would have no reason to fabricate the story. You will understand too, that a fox wouldn't devour a five-month-old foal bar one haunch.' She was so relieved that someone was singing from the same hymn sheet.

'We were hoping that you could show us the whereabouts of the sightings. John can then choose, and decide the best places to put the cameras,' added Ifan.

Caroline took to him straight away, maybe because of his slightly bedraggled Santa Clause, without a sack like appearance.

'I can take you across to our other farm if you like, and show you where our neighbour Tom saw it first, and where mum, James and I saw it on the road, and then where the mares were when Boo was attacked.'

'Boo?'" questioned John, having not uttered a word until now.

'Boo is the name we call the grey mare that was attacked.' said Mary, excited to get involved.

'Are we going there now?' asked Caroline, 'I'll get my boots on if we are, and I'm warning you there is a huge acreage of wilderness between here and Aled's farm which borders ours. There is a network of old mine workings as well. It could be absolutely anywhere. I can show you all the likely pathways though.'

. . .

The rest of Caroline's day was spent trudging through dense undergrowth, uphill, down dale, returning tired and muddied, declaring that she thought Ifan was going to have a heart attack, he was blowing so much going up the steep hills. They had however amid great excitement, discovered paw prints that Ifan was certain belonged to a big cat and not a dog or a fox. He had filled the imprints with liquid silicone after photographing them and returned to them an hour later where the casts had hardened into perfect pads. John had also discovered evidence of score marks, on the bark of a sapling, in the wetland area of land behind the beach café and car park, which he declared were at the right height for a stretching cat.

This area was the first place that John placed a camera. High enough off the ground that a rabbit or fox or cat would not trigger the beam, but it would pick up and film a large wild cat. The little green boxes soon dotted the hillside, at points where the two men reckoned, may be on the pathway a cat may take. Cable tied simply onto branches and thinner sapling trunks. Time would tell they said, if they caught anything. John would be back weekly at least to check on them.

'What do you think it is then, and where would it have come from?' asked Caroline.

'As regards to actual cat species, I'm not a hundred percent certain. I've had a word with some big cat experts, and from the description you've just given me I can go back to them and maybe get a better idea, so tell me again exactly what you saw,' said Ifan. He fumbled in his jacket and bought out a Dictaphone, the same type that James still had in his desk drawer from his newspaper days when he interviewed people.

'Well it was near as dammit black, but the sort of black our old lab goes when he is casting his coat, it takes on a slightly more brownish tinge, and it loses its shine. I would say, a bit like a horse at this time of year who loses that shiny gleam of summer, as its winter coat comes through making it duller. It was much taller and lankier than Ben our Labrador, certainly longer, and it moved with a distinct feline action not a dog's. It was somehow slinking along, its shoulder blades prominent above its shoulders as if it was trying to make itself smaller, his head was very much more cat like, but strong features. The long tail drooped behind, almost as long as its body, the end of it slightly turning up. In fact, it was virtually the width of the single-track lane at the bottom of our fields when it was stretched out.'

Caroline continued now in her enthusiasm. 'It was definitely feline, not a canine, everything about it said cat. It made absolutely no move to be threatening towards us, but actually looked at us for a fair few seconds before it lolloped up the lane, and onwards up the bank. Made the jump up the bank look effortless, and it covered the distance up the slope to the field in just a couple of strides.'

'Wow,' said Ifan. 'You had that good a look at it?' "

'Yes, and Tom next door will tell you the same no doubt. He was sat on his tractor when he saw it that first time, when the police came, he said it nonchalantly backed up to a tree down the bottom wet fields, and seemed to spray like a tom cat would, then walked away towards the bushes behind the beach café.', she continued barely taking a breath.

'A lady along the beach had a horse of hers attacked as well, well at least now she thinks it was attacked, they thought it had been caught in wire a few weeks ago when it happened. It's fly rug was torn to shreds around its quarters and it had cuts there as well. No doubt it would have been worse if the rug hadn't been on it.'

'Mm, may well indicate it is a juvenile then, an adult big cat would have no trouble flooring a horse, and at the end of the day, if you had something like a Panther in the area, you would have people going missing,' said John.

At this comment Caroline nearly choked, spluttering out, 'We had two murders in the area a while back in August, the police are still working on it, though by all accounts they are packing up their stuff at the moment and moving out of the village hall. Locals are saying they have only done half a job as they've have still not got anyone for it. People are only just about starting to relax a bit again, hoping the perpetrator has left the area. Do you think there is any chance at all this could have been the cat? Richard and Margaret who live just up the hill from us said that the injuries were terrible on the young girl. Torn apart, from what Richard described to James.'

She paused for a beat before explaining, 'Richard was the one who found her. Really upset him from what he said. And then there was my friend Jenny, she lives in the forestry. Found someone up a tree when she was out riding. She didn't actually see the man because she ran away, and it was too high. Her horse threw her off, and she was hurt. Oh my God, what do you think?'

'Was that here in this village?' asked Ifan. "I had heard something on the news, but being a mid-Wales man, I'm not that familiar with North Wales locations,' he paused. 'I think we need to ring the police, although I'm sure that they will have thought of this and made the link, won't they?'

'Huh,' butted in John. 'Do you honestly think that they will link it. I'm sure I would, but you never know how much interaction you would get between a CID investigation and a Wildlife Liaison officer, who deals with sheep rustling and stolen osprey eggs and such like.'

Caroline drove them back along the beach, just so that they could see the vast expanse of wild untended acreage there was on the hillside, and that was without including the eighty-seven acres of forestry that covered the hill above Caroline and James's farm.

Chapter Twenty-Four

'WILLIAM EVANS SAT SLUMPED and dishevelled, on the worn horsehair filled chair, by the fireplace. It had once been his mothers, she'd sit on it just like the Queen he believed her to be. Gaping holes now on the armrests, antimacassars long gone, and stuffing exposed and escaping, hosting a wonderful home for the many fleas that inhabited the sitting room, and no doubt a few mice. Yellowing wallpaper hung festooned like Christmas decorations off the walls, meeting the damp line ever spreading wavelike towards them.

The wall above the fireplace blackened by years of open fires, struggling to deposit their acrid wet wood smoke up a blocked chimney. A mixture of brick plaster and crow's nests allowing just a finger of smoke to exit the house. He was well used to the smell by now. In fact, he was probably immune to it, along with the smell of decaying rat bodies, that floated down from the holey roofed attics above. The carpet in the room had long ago been taken up and burnt, only the grime stained black and red quarry tiles now showing. His mother's era in the house clearly long gone. The days were darkening outside, September peeping around the corner and barely six o clock.

Winters he found long and lonely, particularly as his last

remaining sheepdog had been removed by the authorities, alongside his sheep. Too thin, apparently had been the verdict when he had eventually appeared in the Crown court for his prosecution. The local postman had, he believed reported him, no one else really ventured down the drive any more.

He rose from his chair which served now also as his bed, an old threadbare, grey army blanket being used as a cover while he slept, but hardly easing the cold, which seeped through to his bones by the morning. He opened the old fridge door, no longer actually functioning as a fridge. Along with his electric lights, it was turned off permanently since the electricity board switched off his supply for non-payment. He used the fridge to store the few tins of food that he bought from the village shop. He avoided shopping as much as he could. He avoided any interaction with people. Oh, he was fully aware that quite a few people from the village had over the years since his mother died, attempted to help, but it all wore away as he continued to refuse the hand of generosity. He reckoned they were only after any money that his mother may have had.

He opened the can of beans with his trusty pocket knife, the one thing he did take care of, making sure to keep the blade sharp. Devouring the cold contents hungrily he threw the empty can onto the floor. His bath was already full of his cans from previous meals. He had no particular inclination to clear them out.

Grabbing a torch, he opened the back door which over the years had fallen into disrepair. The bottom section of wood, having rotted and fallen away allowing the weather to run amok all around the house. He shone his torch ahead towards the woodshed, rats scurrying away, exposed by the light. Well used to their presence now, they ate any scraps thrown out of the door.

He gathered a couple of logs and threw them down in the entrance porch and returned to the shed where his old dead car lived alongside his slightly less dilapidated Ford pickup, untaxed and uninsured. He topped up the generator at the back with petrol as it whirred and continued to throw out fumes. Looking across to be sure the red light was safely on at the bottom of the old rusting chest freezer, he was relieved to see it still lit. It was his only means of storing a bit of meat for the winter, though now his sheep had gone. There was a time when he used to butcher the odd one himself as needed, normally a sickly ewe, or indeed some he had found already dead. No point in wasting them. The freezer was running at less than half full. It would take him through this winter though, he just needed to make sure it never ran out of petrol and thawed.

Mother had taught him butchering skills, he was still quite a good shot, potting the occasional rabbit, had his shotgun license not been withdrawn along with his twelve- bore shotgun. He was sad at that, it had been his fathers, an old Purdey, one of the first over and under action shotguns designed in the early 1920's. His late father had been a good shot, joining in all the local estate game shoots, rubbing shoulders with the nobility. He died when William was just entering his teens, possibly the greatest loss of his life, no guiding hand, but his mother had taken over that mantle, she raised him like a little prince, and taken care of all the farm's business.

He returned to the house, as cold and damp inside as it was on the outside. He lay a fire shredding, an equally damp and old cattle feed bag, crumpled underneath a single log. The flame slowly took hold. He struggled onto his wellington encased feet, and sat on his chair, his body doing its best to suck the heat from the hearth before it disappeared upstairs and out of the holes in the roof. The rats were still clearly having a party up there.

Chapter Twenty-Five

'JAMES CAME OFF THE PHONE. Caroline, Mary and Emma stood in the kitchen, coffee mugs in hand.

'What did he say?' enquired Caroline.

'Well, at first he laughed, and was full of cocky bluster and police bullshit, but he listened fair play to him. I gave him both Tom and Aled's contact numbers. Told him that Aled was an accountant and Tom a solicitor, as well as both being hobby farmers. I pointed out that they were trustworthy types with no reason to make up stories. I also gave him Dafydd the vet's number so they could have a chat about the injuries. I did phone them earlier, to double check that they were happy for me to give out their mobile numbers, all three were. I'm not sure that he didn't think that we were all mad, but he had obviously read the paper, so he assured me would have a word with the force Wildlife liaison officer, to see if he could find out which officers were on the ground the day Tom first saw it.'

'And did he think that any of this had any relevance in the two murders?' asked Emma.

'Well no, I'm not sure he did, or at least he wasn't going to admit it to me.'

Huws was back in his office, all of the Investigating team having happily moved out of the village hall and back in the warmth of their modern police station. Some of the more specialised members of the team had departed back to their own separate bases. Work was still ongoing on the case, however his boss had declared that they were getting nowhere, not a single confirmed suspect despite costly investigation.

He was annoyed that things like this came down to money, it wasn't as if he had any loose ends he could tie up, nothing, zilch. The Wicker man had defeated him he thought, as he shook his head at no one other than himself.

The cat phone call had come out of the blue and he had initially laughed when he was told about it and had been ready to dismiss it as fantasy, but something at the back of his mind was nagging him. A comment made weeks ago now in the early days of the investigation, he wasn't sure that it was said before the second victim, Morrison had been found. Both these victims were still lying in a mortuary fridge. For the good of the family this needed to be bought to a conclusion.

The thought grew in his head like the workings of a giant computer, his brain stored every bit of information it had been told or seen, even if it had not struck him as important at the time, it would as sure as night turned to day, pop out to the forefront, usually in the dead of night when his brain refused to allow for restful sleep. There it was, the old boy Iorwerth had said something, one simple sentence way back outside the pub, something on the lines of, 'No human has done this.' They may not have been his exact words but near as dammit. He needed to bring him in for a chat, or would that just cause him to clam up? No, he would venture into the pub this evening and hope the old boy was in his usual position at the bar.

Chapter Twenty-Six

IORWERTH WAS ENJOYING his second pint when the hush descended on the room and the policeman walked in. Little clusters immediately congregated in various corners of the pub. Huws nodded at Michael who grabbed a glass from overhead in acknowledgement, wiping it carefully with a tea towel before starting to fill it.

'Evening Iorwerth,' Huws pulled a recently vacated bar stool closer to the old boy, still warm from the hastily removed bottom. 'Can I have a word with you, strictly off the record?'

'Yes, I suppose so, but I don't know any more about anything since you last spoke to me,' he answered gruffly, barely making eye contact.

'No, I appreciate that, but I want to ask you about this big cat that people claim is around.'

Iorwerth sat up at this comment, seemingly prepared to take more interest. 'Yes, there is one, I've seen it with my own eyes on the top road to Beaumaris, I was driving home late one night, and it crossed the road in the light of my headlamps, huge it was. No point telling the authorities about it though, no one would believe you.'

'Are you often out late at night?' asked Huws.

'At this time of year I am. Shooting you see? A couple of us shoot foxes, local farmers pay us per tail. This is the time of year the cubs are out on their own and they do a lot of damage after Christmas come lambing time.' Iorwerth seemed to be relaxing, talking about a subject he understood.

'Have you come across any evidence which might point to the big cat having done some damage?'

"Suppose I have, it's difficult to be know for sure though. For instance, if an ewe lambs' twins at night between the farmers checks, then likely a fox or indeed a cat will take one twin while the ewe is lambing the second, no one would ever know that one is missing, and I don't mean a domestic pussy cat either. A better example would be Eifion's bullock or Caroline's foal. No fox would eat a whole carcase in one night whereas a Panther would do,' said Iorwerth, getting pretty animated now. A subject of interest clearly.

'A panther?' said Huws backing off in surprise. 'Really, what brings you to that conclusion?'

'Well my shooting mate is quite good on the internet stuff, I'm not, I am more of a reader. He looked it up and after Eifion's bullock was found. First of all, he thought it might be some melanistic, or something puma, apparently, that is a cross between a black panther and a beige puma, and the offspring is black. There was a bloke a few years ago now, lived in Llangoed, some sort of Professor at the University. He had big cats in cages in his bloody back garden, had them for years. Talk is that when you had to have a special license to keep animals like that, his wife had them released rather than pay out for new standard cages and provide decent runs for them and stuff. That was back in the mid-seventies though, I doubt those would still be around now, they don't live much longer than fifteen years in captivity, so I doubt it would still be around now having to fend for itself. They do have a territory of around 25 square miles though. Mind you if the originals were male and female, we could be looking at third fourth generation, but to go this long unseen? I doubt it.'

Huws had to admit to himself that he had hugely underestimated the slightly scruffy individual sat across from him, he was no simpleton, far from it. He found a new respect for old Iorwerth. Gwen his wife had always accused him of being too quick to judge people and treat everyone as a criminal until proven otherwise. He needed to heed her advice more often.

'I want to ask you really about a comment you made to me outside the pub a couple of days after Sarah Jones's body was found, do you remember?' He went on, 'You said words to the effect of, no human could do that.'

Iorwerth nodded slowly and deliberately taking a last dredge of his pint. Huws looked towards Michael and indicated another pint for the old boy.

'Yes, I remember, the first thing that came into my head when it got out in the village what the injuries had looked like, I thought big cat, even then. When that poor man was found in the tree, we thought straight away that it would be the cat, a bloody big cat to drag someone up there.'

Huws sat head down, he had people to talk to, sooner rather than later.

'Thank you Iorwerth, I appreciate you talking to me, it was most helpful, and you have obviously done your homework on the subject. You be careful now when you are out shooting, you never know what you might meet.'

'Oh, we have already met by torchlight. I knew it was the cat, bright yellow eyes, too far apart to be anything smaller, foxes and other animals tend to be a greenish or even a reddish shade when they reflect back at you. I had it in my sights,' muttered Iorwerth.

'Why didn't you shoot it?' he asked. 'Why would I? everything has the right to live, but things have changed a bit since the two bodies were found, for whatever reason it has clearly started to stalk humans, that's why we are out at night. James down the road asked us to as well, after they lost the foal.'

'Three bodies,' corrected Huws. 'This may well put a different perspective on the remains found at the quarry too.'

'Yes, I can understand that,' agreed Iorwerth.

Huws hoped to God that Emyr Rowlands had kept decent records of the autopsies because it looked like he was going to need them.

Chapter Twenty-Seven

ROWLANDS WASN'T best pleased to be receiving a call during a family celebratory meal. His family had arranged a surprise birthday dinner. He wasn't one for parties, so a quiet restaurant meal had suited him.

'Can this not wait till morning? Particularly as you don't seem to have another victim for me, I can appreciate your concern, but I'm sure it can wait.'

'Yes, yes okay I agree.' Huws accepted he was being just a tad exigent.

He placed the phone back in his pocket and sat at the table that Gwen had laid for his tea. Fair play to her, she had fully taken on the often-mad timetable of his job since he was promoted. No regular shift patterns now, sometimes barely putting his head down whilst working a case, other than a quick snooze if he was lucky enough to have a comfy office chair, which in these last few weeks had certainly not been the case, in the chill of the village hall. Thank God he thought, he was working out of his normal office at the moment. Suppers were often reheated affairs in this house, but despite this she always made sure he was well fed when he was there. She had less control of any rubbish he might consume in his hours of work though.

'Any developments today, that you can tell me about?' asked Gwen. She knew full well that her husband rarely bought his work home. He never had. Often the only way she found out about anything would be if she heard village gossip or read it in the papers. Gossip was not normally something she was involved with, even in her monthly ladies' group or her weekly writing group, she would rarely be included in anything that people feared she may take home to her husband.

Sometimes being a Detective Inspectors wife was a burden, sometimes it put pressure on her as she was considered a worthy lady to open village fetes and such like. Always being invited onto some committee or other. She didn't mind this too much as it actually did give her some order in her life and regular happenings, the polar opposites to her home life with her husband. Ifan, exhaled forcibly and leant back on the dining chair.

He put his cutlery down and said 'Uum, yes, well a cat, a big cat, I think a big wild cat has been responsible for what we thought were murders. A few people have seen it and there have been suspicious large animal losses due to it, or so the locals believe. There has been a bit of a cloak of secrecy around it, maybe for years, people scared of being laughed at and made to feel like their imagination has run wild.

The first time it was seen in recent times, our force wildlife officer put the sighting down to a badger, the dingbat. All our work the last few weeks, if this is indeed the case, a total waste of time. No wonder we haven't come up with anything concrete. I'm not looking forward to telling the Chief Inspector, he has been on my back regarding this case as it is. He says the usual, this is costing a lot of money and you have got nowhere speech.'

Gwen sat silent. She didn't know if she was more shocked by the cat aspect which sounded quite plausible, or sad that the case was clearly having such a negative effect on her husband, she hadn't been aware that the Chief Inspector was pressurising him to this extent, but she supposed that there wasn't a bottomless purse for these things.

'How are you going to play it from now?' she asked.

'I'm meeting Emyr tomorrow morning, Emyr Rowlands the pathologist. He did the autopsies on the three victims. Well two, we had already declared on his say so that the skeletal remains at the quarry had more than likely been a suicide. We found the likely missing person through the database, all the suspicions correlated, mental health issues and so on, and he assumed as we did, that the body had been picked clean over time by carrion, foxes, domestic cats maybe, and then insect life and general decomposition in weather and tide. The family have buried him now.

I hope to god that Emyr has some decent photos and notes on the case, or we will be looking at exhuming his body. For the family's sake I pray it doesn't come to that.

Now, we have had such positive sightings of a big cat by some pretty sensible professionals, we need to look at the other victims again to see if the actual reason for their death, could in fact be attributed to a big cat attack.'

He continued, sounding exhausted, his supper cooling by the minute before him. 'A fair few cameras, night vision, special ones have been put up by some BBC wildlife people, so it will be interesting to see if anything comes of that. I'm also going to have to bring in all the people who claim to have seen it, so we can get individual statements regarding its description and tomorrow, I will see about maybe talking to some big cat experts, Chester zoo, London Zoo, Longleat, anywhere really where we might get expert advice regards what animal we are talking about and its likely behaviour.

It worries me that even if it has been around a while, it's now got itself a taste for human flesh, and with winter virtually on top of us, it may get hungry and actually start tracking and stalking people.

They have a huge territory range apparently; it could well be comfortably wandering around the whole east side of Anglesey and possibly further west. Apparently, a jogger in Capel Gwyn, near Bryngwran now claims to have seen it, running alongside him on the other side of a wall, pacing him, step for step'.

He picked up his cutlery and started on his supper, they ate in silence. It would be a restless night's sleep tonight.

Chapter Twenty-Eight

AT FEW MINUTES TO NINE, Huws was waiting in the back office of the Mortuary suite. Rowlands swept in followed by Jane, who had presided over the original autopsies.

'Right, ok, let's see if I have got this right. Despite all our forensic tests and examinations, and hundreds of results, you have drawn no conclusions whatsoever that would give us a murderer in the case of these two victims?' asked Rowlands as Huws butted in.

'Three, this draws suspicions that the skeletal remains that were found in the quarry, is not as we first thought, a suicide, it's now possibly linked to the other two.' Rowlands looked at him over his glasses.

'You think these victims may have met their unfortunate demise at the teeth and claws of a big cat? Are your superiors singing from the same hymn sheet?'

'No, not as yet, in fact this isn't open knowledge yet, I haven't approached the Chief with this new angle, I want you to have a second look at the two we still have here, to see if there could have been a possibility that the injuries had been caused by an animal, and hopefully you will have enough photos from the autopsy of the more decomposed victim whose body was released.

I'm sure you said something at the time, that there were deep unusual serrations on the femur bone, that was then put down to weathering due to exposure. Would you think maybe, they could have been inflicted by an animal such as a big cat, actually holding down a leg as it was eating? You also said-', Huws looked at his note book now. 'Soft tissue tendon and muscle had decomposed completely, and only fibrous ligamentous tissue held some of the bones together, particularly in the lower legs. Could that be because they were chewed off as opposed to decaying?'

As the words left his mouth, Huws felt as if he were in some surreal world, describing the sort of stuff that only occurs in the most bizarre of nightmares. He believed looking at Rowlands that he thought the same.

'Come on man, do you really believe this tosh? Grant you, the injuries inflicted were not normal, to what we would expect to see, but a big cat? Jane, put the kettle on please, we have some talking to do'.

Over the next two hours, every thread of possibility was discussed and double checked, photos, autopsy details, and finally as Huws had expected, but not looked forwards to, the two victim's bodies. The bodies had been stored in a made for purpose forensic refrigerator.

Huws even remembered Rowlands telling him a number of years before of his new facility. This refrigerated room, allowed the body to be kept at a negative temperature, unlike the normal hospital mortuaries which were for shorter periods similar to a household fridge. The negative temperature although not freezing the bodies would certainly slow down the rate of decomposition. Both bodies were coated in a light powder, it's purpose Rowlands explained, to prevent any bacterial growths. They looked slightly gaunter, the skin having a certain sheen to it. Morrisons face was covered by a special sheet of skin like, skin coloured plastic, which at least hid the horrendous damage that he had sustained.

Rowlands and Jane checked and double checked every aspect against a computer screen on the wall, which not only gave an enlarged view of what they were seeing, but at a touch of a button, previously taken photographs, numerical graphs and result tables appeared.

The conclusion was finally drawn, over a coffee, that Rowlands did agree that the cause of death could be a big cat attack. He agreed to put his professional reputation and name to a declaration saying so.

'Do you remember the drink you had and vomited out, immediately after the first autopsy? Well as long as you promise not to waste a good tot of Lagavulin, I'll get you another'.

He poured out three measures, Jane once again like on the previous occasion, joining them once she had cleared the tables and replaced the bodies one above the other on their shelves in the fridges.

'What do we do now?' uttered Huws.

'Well, that isn't really a question for me is it? I'm happy to give a cause of death, but proof? In all honesty you need proof and I'm not at all sure how you are going to get that, until you actually have the thing in front of you for all to see.'

'There are men out looking every night, but I'm not sure how long that will carry on for before the novelty wears off, and if you knew the area where it has been seen, then it's like looking for a needle in the proverbial haystack. One old boy that I have spoken to has had it in the sights of its gun but didn't see reason to shoot it. There is bound to be a reaction from the anti-hunting brigade. The distance between the victim in the tree and the quarry is probably three miles, with the young girl's body somewhere in the middle. Their range is huge. I had a chat in the early hours of this morning with a big cat curator from Chester Zoo. He didn't seem surprised to hear of the cat, saying that it was known that there were probably, over a hundred big cats roaming in the countryside in the UK, along with wallabies, Racoons, American mink and Parakeets, most having escaped from captivity, and often denied, from fear of repercussions, by illegal owners.

It was a big thing at one time for owners of stately homes to own lions and tigers. Most of these however were handed over to zoo's when the laws changed.

He also said, and this is the worrying thing, it's likely old or injured. One or the other will mean it is unable to stalk normal prey, which it would have been doing, lambs, rabbits, ground nesting birds, cats, small dogs if given the opportunity, but being older and less efficient a hunter, may have led it to be hungry.

They don't eat daily, in the wild they may eat a deer, or wild boar a week, between those as a snack, they may eat smaller things like armadillos in the wild. However, being a poor hunter may well mean it turning its sights to easier prey. A healthy adult cat would never purposely be seen by us, they are just too secretive for that he reckoned.

Here on Anglesey for instance, no walker would expect to come across a big cat on a public footpath through the woods. However, in his opinion, you could in fact walk as close as ten feet away, from a well-hidden big cat, and have absolutely no idea that it was there. It also explains the types of injuries inflicted both in the initial kill, and in how the kill was devoured. The cat may well have been disturbed he reckoned, when it killed the male victim hence it dragged him up into a tree. An easy task apparently for a creature such as a Panther. The only other animals who could do that would likely be lions or Tigers, particularly of the Sumatran variety who were known to stalk their potential victims, sometimes for days, in remote villages. Siberian Tigers are pretty big. The description given though, points towards a Panther.'

'Shit,' said Jane who had joined them at the beginning of this description. 'I won't be walking in the woods anytime soon; I'm out walking every chance I get!'

It was a very subdued Huws, that walked into his office at lunchtime. No matter which way he played it in his head, he was going to have to tell his team that Sarah Jones, Philip Morrison and the lad from Barmouth had more than likely been attacked, killed and partially eaten by a big cat. But tell them he did.

You could have heard a pin drop in the room such was the reaction, until one young CID rookie laughed out loud.

'Are you having a laugh Sir? A big Cat, surely the locals have had one too many magic mushrooms at a party, and come up with a fairy story? All the work we have put in, all the house to house investigations, the phone calls to every man and his dog, we'll be a laughing stock.'

Huws let him have his rant and watched as others clearly agreed with him, nodding their heads.

He passed a memory stick to PC Howard, 'Can you put this up on the screen?' Within minutes autopsy photographs appeared on the screen of all three victims. Huws for the next hour laboriously went through them, notebook in hand, filling them all in on Rowlands' comments and opinions which could very well tie these up with a cat attack.

'Right, next job, while I go and talk to the Chief and try to persuade him that what we have found is plausible, I want you to go through each and every search case on Anglesey in the last five, no ten years, and tie up autopsy cases to any bodies that were found, see if there are any possibilities that any others could actually have been killed in the same way. It's unlikely, as the Zoo bloke feels this is the result of an old or injured animal, but we want to cover all our bases. Also, I want you to get onto a guy called John Thompson, here is his number.'

Huws wrote the number on a scrap of paper and passed it to a still dumbfounded WPC. 'Ask him to check his wildlife cameras that they set up. I know it's only a couple of days, if that, but they have been up overnight now at least, and if the animal is still in the area of its latest kill, they may have picked it up on one of the cameras.'

He was on a roll now, having gone from not having a clue what he was going to say, to having plans coming out of him like after vindaloo diarrhoea. 'One of you contact the Daily post. They did a story on this a few days ago, we need to confirm that we, as the Police, come up with a response to this situation without making ourselves look like a load of numpties and scaremongers.

We need to get a press release out which asks people to be vigilant, preferably not going out alone to anywhere remote, and be very careful and aware of their immediate surroundings. I'm going to ask if we can have the helicopter up a few times with its FLIR device, to see if it can pick up anything remotely panther like in the area of Wern y Wylan, the forestry behind, and the woodland between Wern and Allt Goch which is a vast area. Maybe a sweep around the quarries along the coast towards Penmon too, though apparently there aren't as many places to hide. Cave rescue hopefully will have an explore in the caves, of the old mines between Wern woods, and Allt Goch.'

'Wow, fancy going into a cave and coming across a panther,' said a voice from the back. Papers were shuffled, phones were dialled, Huws, left the room and prepared for his chat with the Chief. This will be fun, he thought as he straightened his tie.

Chapter Twenty-Nine

AUTUMN MOVED INEVITABLY INTO WINTER. The Chief Inspector had almost choked on his tea, when Huws suggested that the murders were actually caused by a wild cat. Rowlands the pathologist had confirmed, that having looked again with a totally different viewpoint, his conclusions were that the damage could have been caused by a large predator, in this case the black cat which had been seen.

The case was closed as far as the police were concerned. Relatives, although aghast initially at the conclusion, had accepted it and had been allowed to put their loved ones to rest. Life went on. Anglesey, became a hive of big cat activity, every man and his dog had seen it. Rhosneigr, Dulas, Parys Mountain, Capel Gwyn, Newborough, the hills around Llanfairynghornwy, you name it, it had been seen there.

The worrying aspect was that a couple of people claimed to have seen two. Research on the subject claimed that a cat in captivity might if it were lucky, survive for twenty years, however a cat released into an environment such as onto the island, would more than likely live for closer to eight to twelve years if it wasn't captured or shot. It gave the game shooting enthusiasts something totally different to hunt over the winter months.

The zoo experts were worried about this aspect, worrying that a glance off shot, as opposed to a kill, might in fact render an animal less capable of hunting, therefore making it hungrier and more likely to take another chance at a human. Some people who had first hand sightings of it slightly changed their life patterns.

Caroline and James were now very wary of using some of their hillier landlocked fields, bordering Wern woods. Jenny up in the forestry, stuck to the open tracks whilst hacking out, rather than veering off into the darker corners of the woods. Mountain bike enthusiasts were now tending to seek the thrill of the forestry tracks in groups, as opposed to alone, and generally the local farmers were more aware that they may have more than a fox to worry about.

Obviously, there were still the sceptics, but woe betide anyone in the local pub who tried to belittle Iorwerth and his sightings. He had become a bit of a celebrity in the retelling of his story to anyone who asked. In fact, the whole thing seemed to have created a small group of believers who lived in a slightly parallel world, who spoke amongst each other but chose not to openly discuss it for fear of being ridiculed.

The one person who in fact had anything like proof from that winter was Caroline, the only person with an actual photo, taken through her kitchen window when she had been washing up. An actual picture of the cat crossing a short bridge over a ditch in their back field, casually, as if it had all the time in the world. The photograph had been sent to a big cat expert, and verified to be a melanistic puma, likely full grown and elderly. By its coat which lacked a healthy lustre, it likely was not managing to hunt efficiently as suspected, hence why it had stalked humans. Whether it was a temporary blip and it had recovered from sickness of some sort, would probably never be known until it was captured dead or alive.

However, Caroline had an even more frightening encounter with it in the late winter, after the killings when she was woken from sleep to hear the horses noisily whinnying and clearly banging their stable doors. She ventured out in welly boots and dressing-gown to check, lest one of the animals was colicing, only to encounter the big cat standing sideways on, no more than fifteen feet or so away from her. Random advice gleaned from watching a Sir David Attenborough TV programme, regarding encounters with Grizzly bears in the wild, led her to raise her hands in the air, stand on tip toes and slowly retreat backwards. Make yourself look big he said, being only five foot three that was quite a challenge, and she couldn't remember whether she was supposed to maintain eye contact or not.

The cat made no indication that it was going to attack. She was rescued from the feed-room shortly after by a father and sister, armed with coal shovels banging the sides of the shed as they approached. Clearly the sight of Caroline in her dressing-gown had been too much for it.

Winter became spring, the village and Anglesey in general slipped back into its normal rhythms, people started walking the footpaths and lanes of the area once more, alone and in groups. The sceptics having already forgotten and some believing the police negligent and foolhardy, to have closed what they believed to be a murder case with the guilty party still likely to be on the loose, local, people putting blame on the weirder inhabitants of the locality, the loners and the unsociables.

Character traits like this were always picked up on in rural communities, where everyone reckoned to know everyone's business. Maybe someone waiting on the next opportunity. Only time would tell.

Chapter Thirty

THE COASTGUARD SERVICE continued to have callouts and training sessions, the inevitable searches for missing persons, one of the less pleasurable tasks asked of the teams. People would always be going missing, it was the nature of human beings, things happened to them within family circles, marriage breakdowns, mental health issues, drug and alcohol abuse and dependency, and as had probably always been, and poorly recognised, post-traumatic stress disorder, still not receiving the attention it should have.

Some people were never found, some people never wanted to be found. They were added by the police to the missing persons database as failed finds, friends and loved ones destined to a life of hope that one day they would be found alive, or even dead, that, at least gave closure. The team local to Allt Goch had for a time, been a little cautious if the search was centred around the so-called big cats' territory, but nothing suspicious arose to make them think there was any animal involvement. Ceri however, refused point blank to search anywhere unless there were at least two of her buddies with her, and tended to be the noisiest coastguard on the team, in order she claimed to frighten a cat away. Tomos though reckoned that any big cat would take one look at a feisty Ceri and not dare attack her.

Their search methods of sweeping ahead with a torch, left and right, and then behind themselves to cover the track from another perspective, always made Ceri nervous just in-case she was being followed, but she was quite confident that if Tomos released one of his totally toxic farts, it would instantly kill the cat.

Pub life carried on, the choir had been allowed back into their village hall, the various chess, dog training, knitting, and reading clubs had slipped back into their routines like feet into old slippers at the end of a long day.

Chapter Thirty-One

WILLIAM EVANS in his own grumpy way enjoyed the spring. It wasn't quite the same now that his sheep had gone, but it did allow him to catch a few more rabbits for the pots. He used the old-fashioned snare method, knowing full well it was considered cruel, but he checked the snares two to three times a day, the rabbits never suffering for long before he dispatched them. He would though feel inordinately cruel when he found a Doe in the snare who was in milk, understanding that the kits would no doubt, at this time of year starve, and perish inside their burrows. He would skin and quarter them and add them to whatever he happened to have stewing in the pot on the fire.

The only aspect of the spring that he didn't like, was the increase in backpacked strangers that crossed his land. They had the perfect right to, he knew that full well, there were mapped public footpaths, but he still saw it as an intrusion on his privacy. He had never understood the need by some people to trudge around the countryside, particularly crossing what was obviously private farmed land, disturbing stock and making farmers feel the need to be careful as to what they grazed in a particular field, particularly bulls. In his opinion though bulls were often less harmless than a field of newly calved cows, they could give anyone a run for their money protecting their calves.

Mother had never minded, in fact she had always left some scones or Bara-brith in a small open fronted shed by the gate, along with some eggs. There was an honesty box, it was quite surprising how much pin money she made in a good week. That was until some of the local youths actually cottoned on to a cash supply and started walking down the lane to steal the contents. This saddened his mother, who continued to put in her offerings for a while before giving up. The shed still stood, forlorn and dilapidated at the top of the drive, empty now. He had no hens since the last bedraggled Rhode Island red had died and he certainly was not inclined to cook scones any time soon.

He visited town the other day and although the odd person knew him and acknowledged him, it was certainly not a social visit. He purchased a couple of loaves which he would chuck in the freezer in the shed, a few tins of beans to keep him going over the next week, and unusually for him, a few potatoes and a pot of granules to make some gravy. He listened in to chatter whilst he waited to pay in the queue, talk was of a local big cat which was now believed to be the guilty party in what had been thought to have been two, likely three deaths.

He was pleased to receive knowledge of this news. He could have told people years ago that the cat was about. Living where he did, it was a regular visitor which he had crossed paths with on numerous occasions. Choosing no longer to mow the fields, the pastures had grown into tussocks of new growth over old for quite a while. Yellow ragwort making its way upwards and reseeding and spreading year on year as did the docks, nettles and Fat hen. Flattened tracks criss-crossed the fields, the regular motorways of foxes and no doubt on occasion this cat. There were some flattened areas where an animal would obviously have lain and rested. He had in fact taken to throwing the odd rabbit into the field if his snares had captured a rabbit too many. Another wasteful act, and he supposed that he should in reality just put them in the freezer, for less fruitful times.

He had never felt threatened by the cat, assuming that at one time in its life it likely lived alongside human's albeit in a secure cage. It was an animal he was thankful for as it had allowed him to have a few more guilty pleasures in life, than he may have done since the time his dear old mother was alive. No point making a song and dance about it. Until now it was unlikely anyone would have believed him. Today, he would re-lay his fire and get it going well, would place the old iron griddle wire across the heat once the fire had settled and died down, when satisfied he would place the meat onto the griddle and cook it through, some for tonight with a baked potato and gravy, and maybe it would last him a few days with a bit of bread. This meat supply would last him through the year if he were lucky, he would then need to find another chance like the last one to take him through other years. He would need to be make sure he never got careless. The quarry was one of his local haunts, remote, quiet, though there was talk recently of adding it as a scenic route to the local section of the coastal path, bloody foot-paths again. Rabbits bred by the dozen down there, that was the main reason he originally went down there, long before the big cat came on the scene.

The poor man that he encountered down there, didn't have a chance against him, being that he was a towering bear of a man. Bloody do gooder townie, he had been sitting there off his head on whatever drugs he had taken. William was not wise to the drug ways of the world, he had no experience of alcohol either, his mother had always been vehemently against it, mainly due to her own father having killed himself through drink.

The man actually had the cheek to start ranting at him for his cruelty. Dispatching rabbits was quick, as humane as he could make it, if there was such a thing as humane slaughter. He had even offered the bloke one to cook up on the beach stones, loads of drift-wood around he had suggested, but oh no, he just ranted about all creatures being equal. It was because of people like him, who had absolutely no moral code, that the world had become as it was. William was quite naïve to these ways he referred to, not having a television or ever reading a paper. The only thing he read was his mother's old Bible occasionally. Suddenly spittle covered Williams' face as he was prodded and poked repeatedly in the chest by the stranger's forefinger. William stood his ground for a while in disbelief rather at the ranting. The rage continued, he involved God, and how William was clearly a disgrace before God for thinking he could willy-nilly kill creatures as he felt inclined. He then accused William of being an embarrassment to his mother.

It all happened in a flash, the penknife entered his neck just below the ear and cut towards the vulnerable centre of the neck, cutting across vessels which gurgled blood over and down the man's shirt collar. A look of disbelief and utter surprise, before the eyes emptied, a look that William reckoned he would never forget. The man fell to his knee's as if praying to the giant of a man before him, but he was already dead, when he slipped to the ground. William looked around, knowing there would be no one to have viewed this atrocity. He needed to think quickly. What would his mother do now? What a stupid thing to think, his mother would never have done such a thing, but she loved her son above all else, she would no doubt have a solution for his situation.

William dragged the man up behind the old stone dressing sheds, roofless now but still a few concealed corners to carry out the next stage of this awful plan. Bleeding an animal is important after death or it taints the meat, he had a length of rope that he used to tie up the neck of the old hessian sack, that he carried his rabbits it. He tied the man's ankles together, then dragged him to the rusting metal framework of the shed where the brickwork had collapsed. His head thumping roughly over the pebbles and bigger rocks. William knew it wouldn't be hurting him now.

Throwing the end of the rope over a beam; he had checked it held his own weight by hanging off it. With difficulty and a lot of grunting, he pulled the weight equivalent he reckoned to a well grown two-month-old Friesian bull calf. The man hung by his feet in a grizzly upside- down hanging sort of position. Williams assumed that even though he was dead, like a Sunday dinner cockerel he would drip out his life blood, or like the pigs that had been hung in the old sheds. Blood, then valued, and saved for the preparation of black pudding, every part of the pig used. He would aim to do the same. No waste. His mother had been in the habit of re-presenting a cold unfinished previous meal in front of him, should he leave food on his plate.

It took him two days to cut him up into joints, he left the arms and the head, three separate journeys did he make, up and down the hill and across the fields mainly by the light of the moon, returning home to his freezer like a sinister Father Christmas without the hat and beard. Between visits, he had covered the body in a sack, to prevent attack by birds and foxes, though he suspected that the rats may well have had a nibble through the night.

Task completed. He had stripped the meat off the bone, keeping the skeleton intact, he had even re dressed the man. He then cut him down, placing him behind the building, a nightmare vision in empty jeans and shirt. A Rictus grin, jaw dropped, already hollowing cheeks looking back at him, half shut empty eye almost staring in judgemental disbelief. The other eye had clearly provided a meal for a scavenging carrion crow. This vision he imagined would live with him for a long time.

At home by candlelight, he had rolled up the meat from the legs, the abdomen and the back, creating what he believed looked very similar to a rolled joint expertly tied by a butcher, all skills taught to him as a young boy by his mother. Surplus strips of meat he had put through the old mincer. In his mother's day, given a surplus of intestinal tissue, the mince would have created reams of sausages. He would have to make do with mince. He had not been able to strip the arms, he felt slightly sick at the thought of the skin still having the sleeve of tattoos on, he couldn't use that.

The remains had eventually been discovered many months after, he had in fact enjoyed the proceeds of his cleverness on many an evening, before the two kayakers had found the man, all scraps of flesh by then disintegrated and eaten by various creatures. Just a partly clothed sun and wind bleached grinning skeleton remained, still the same grin, a few ligaments still hanging on like gnarled yellow ropes. He knew this, because over the period of time since the dispatch and the discovery he had silently walked down to the quarry to monitor the level of decomposition, in fact he had found the whole process fascinating.

It was quite amusing to William, to hear that the man had indeed been identified, and like the other two genuine cat killings the other side of the village, this was believed to have been the same.

Unfortunately, for William Evans, his frozen meat supply was going to eventually come to an end.

He wasn't too worried about this now, after all, the cat was still around, as were the damned nuisance ramblers. He would no doubt get his chance again, he had killed once, surely, it couldn't be that difficult, to do it again.

Afterword

Facts on the fiction

This book has been written by a woman, who has had many personal sightings on her own land, and local area of a big cat, as have her neighbours and friends. Her theory is that the only way it could be there, is that a captive wild cat, has at some time been released and adapted itself to living wild. It has not in reality harmed anyone, unlike the Cat in this book. That is a pure figment of the authors imagination as is the twist in the 'tail'. Only time would tell on that score. The locals in general will know of the sightings, some adamant in their descriptions, others sceptical.

The village the book is based on is a place that sprawls along a vast wooded hillside, its western end covered in a forest, hundreds of acres of neglected wild land, criss-crossed by pathways and tracks. The lower parts of the village spreads out onto ten square miles of beach. Woodlands hide a network of ancient blocked by and large mine workings, semi hidden by self-seeded sycamore saplings.

The authors smallholding was at the centre of the length of the beach, one of the primary locations of the actual sightings. The horse attacks are real, as is the loss of the bullock, the human attacks are a work of fiction.

Years have passed now since the last sighting in the area, however at the time of publishing, there was a recent sighting more to the east of the island. If it's the same cat that was seen in the early two thousands, it will be a very old cat by now. It is hoped that there are not more on the island. The BBC wildlife camera side is real, cameras were set up. The newspaper reports at the time are also real as is the only photograph that was taken of the animal.

The author hopes that whatever its demise, or in fact if it still alive, that it has had a happy existence on our beautiful island.

Acknowledgments

This book is fiction based on fact, which will make itself apparent as the tale develops. All names used are fictional but most places do exist. People may well imagine they recognise themselves in the story and I thank all the people who were actually involved alongside me in the true parts of the tale; my parents and sister and business partner who also witnessed various scenes from this book. Also huge thanks must go to my step-grandaughter Hayley, yet again, for helping me with the more technical aspects of book publishing.

About the Author

The author lives on the island of Anglesey off North Wales, her interests are the outdoors, walking the coast and hills. She was previously a college lecturer and a Coach and examiner for The British Horse Society. She now Trains people in First Aid Skills and has been an Active Coastguard volunteer for 21 years to date.

Her main love was her horse breeding business alongside her late husband and business partner, being one of the few Artificial Insemination Technicians at the time. She now spends her time teaching, looking after her remaining geriatric brood mares and rescue hens, and turning out when her pager goes off, whilst dreaming of writing novels on jaunts in the campervan.

We can all dream.

She has drawn on her experiences of many aspects of life to write this book. Her previous published works have been mainly equestrian journalism and a children's story 'On the Run' also about the Cat.

Also by Anne Roberts

DI Huws Book 2 Community Secrets and Lies

DI Huws Book 3 Community Confessions

On the Run- a stand alone short story